The Trial of God

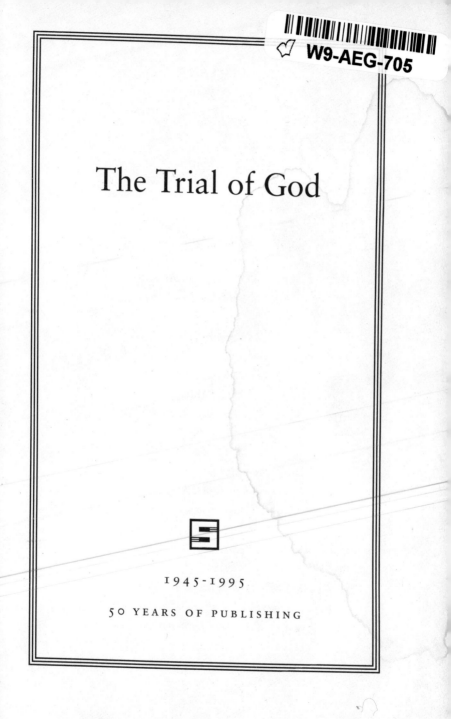

1945-1995

50 YEARS OF PUBLISHING

BOOKS BY
Elie Wiesel

Night

Dawn

The Accident

The Town Beyond the Wall

The Gates of the Forest

The Jews of Silence

Legends of Our Time

A Beggar in Jerusalem

One Generation After

Souls on Fire

The Oath

Ani Maamin (cantata)

Zalmen, or the Madness of God (play)

Messengers of God

A Jew Today

Four Hasidic Masters

The Trial of God (play)

The Testament

Five Biblical Portraits

Somewhere a Master

The Golem (illustrated by Mark Podwal)

The Fifth Son

Against Silence (edited by Irving Abrahamson)

Twilight

The Six Days of Destruction (with Albert Friedlander)

From the Kingdom of Memory

Sages and Dreamers

The Forgotten

The Trial of God

(as it was held on February 25, 1649, in Shamgorod)

═══

A Play by

Elie Wiesel

Translated by
Marion Wiesel

Introduction by Robert McAfee Brown

Afterword by Matthew Fox

Schocken Books
NEW YORK

Library of Congress Cataloging-in-Publication Data

Wiesel, Elie, 1928-
[Procès de Shamgorod tel qu'il se déroula le 25 février 1649. English]
The trial of God (as it was held on February 25, 1649, in Shamgorod) : a play /
by Elie Wiesel ; translated by Marion Wiesel ; introduction by Robert McAfee
Brown ; afterword by Matthew Fox.
p. cm.
ISBN 0-8052-1053-9
1. Gezerot takh ve-tat, 1648-1649—Drama. 2. Jews—Persecutions—
Ukraine—Drama. 3. Ukraine—History—1648-1654—Drama. I. Title.
PQ2683.I32P7613 1995
842—dc20   95-20799
CIP

Manufactured in the United States of America
First Schocken edition published in 1986
2 4 6 8 ['95]9 7 5 3 1

For Professor Louis Finkelstein

INTRODUCTION

by Robert McAfee Brown

By the time he was fifteen, Elie Wiesel was in Auschwitz, a
Nazi death camp. A teacher of Talmud befriended him by insist-
ing that whenever they were together they would study Talmud—Talmud without pens or pencils, Talmud without paper,
Talmud without books. It would be their act of religious defiance.

Once night the teacher took Wiesel back to his own barracks,
and there, with the young boy as the only witness, three great
Jewish scholars—masters of Talmud, Halakhah, and Jewish ju-
risprudence—put God on trial, creating, in that eerie place, "a
rabbinic court of law to indict the Almighty."[1] The trial lasted
several nights. Witnesses were heard, evidence was gathered,
conclusions were drawn, all of which issued finally in a unani-
mous verdict: the Lord God Almighty, Creator of Heaven and
Earth, was found *guilty* of crimes against creation and humankind. And then, after what Wiesel describes as an "infinity
of silence," the Talmudic scholar looked at the sky and said "It's
time for evening prayers," and the members of the tribunal re-
cited Maariv, the evening service.

For years Wiesel lived with the tension and dilemma of that
memory, pondering how to communicate its despairing solem-
nity. Nothing "worked." It did not work as a novel, it did not
work as a play, it did not even work as a cantata. Each successive
manuscript ended up in a desk drawer. (Wiesel admits to having
a large desk drawer.) Finally, he took the event out of the present, resituated it in the past, just after the widespread Chmiel-
nicki pogroms in the years of 1648–49, and turned it into a
Purimschpiel (a play to be enacted on the feast of Purim), although one written in the style of a "tragic farce."

Purim is a festive holiday in the Jewish liturgical year.[2] It celebrates a Jewish victory over anti-Semitism, recounted in the Hebrew Scriptures in the book of Esther.[3] It is a baldly "secular" story, in which the name of God is never even mentioned. Since there are so few Jewish victories to celebrate, the holiday of Purim is a special favorite—a time for unabashed levity, augmented with masks, noisemakers, whistles for heroes (and heroines), boos, derision of villains as they appear in the retelling of the tale, all accompanied by lots of eating and, as becomes increasingly evident during the evening, lots of drinking. There are many Jews for whom it is a religious obligation to get drunk on Purim. Another frequent activity is the production of a play, a *Purimschpiel*, with an exaggerated style of humor that is by turns absurd, ridiculous, unlikely, and satirical. But as the action of *The Trial of God* progresses—the result is "a *Purimschpiel* within a *Purimschpiel*"—we discover that that levity can give way to deadly seriousness.

If, as David Blumenthal argues in *Facing the Abusing God*,[4] Wiesel's play "is a modern rereading of the Book of Job," it is also a rereading of the book of Jeremiah, many of the Psalms, and much of the tradition, all of which are centrally expressing the cry, "Why?" Why the death of my daughter? Why the slaughter of whole towns and villages? Why the killing that is not a routine but is rather designed to prolong the suffering and pain? Why a God in whose name such things are not only done, but done exultantly? Surely any God worthy of the name would not only refuse to condone such brutality but would expend all of the divine effort necessary to bring the brutality to a halt, and initiate the work of passionate rebuilding.

The foundation of the plot of *The Trial of God* is best described by Wiesel himself in this bare-bones summary, which he prepared for an address given at Loyola University, in Chicago, in 1980:

What is the story? Three minstrels, three *Purim spielers*, come to a city called Shamgorod in the Ukraine. It is Purim eve, and they want to perform a play in order to get food and drink. The innkeeper says, "Are you crazy?

Don't you know where you are? You are in Shamgorod. There was a pogrom here last year. Everyone was killed. I and my daughter are the only Jews here. And you want to perform here?" They insist on performing and finally he says, "All right. Under one condition—that I will give you the idea. The theme will be a *din torah* with God, a trial of God. I want you to indict God for what he has done to my family, to my community, to all these Jews." The hungry performers accept.

In the first act the decision is made to hold a trial. In the second act there is a problem; nobody wants to play the role of God's attorney. In the third act we have the trial itself.[5]

Let us begin by examining issues raised by some of the subordinate characters and then concentrate on the clash between Berish, the innkeeper, who insistently calls God to account, and Sam, who defends God against all charges.

There is Maria, the tough and shrewd maid at the inn. When Sam, whoever he is, finally appears at the end of Act II, she screams, recognizing him as a man who came to the inn, seduced her with endearing and comforting words she was unwise enough to believe, and after he had worked his will on her, denounced her as a common slut. Her moments describing the seduction are gentle and even beautiful, for she had believed his protestations of love. The notion that *this* man, whom she calls "Satan," would become the defense attorney for God appalls her, and she works, unsuccessfully, to have him disqualified. She fears that he will fool the rest of the court as he has already fooled her. Her fears are well founded.

Mendel, one of the Purim minstrels, is noteworthy for his depth and thoughtfulness, and is a natural choice to be judge at the trial of God. He is secretive about his background, and frequently asks the question, "And God in all of this?" We learn finally that, like Berish, he was one of the few survivors of an earlier pogrom in which he thinks he saw Sam.

But even he, as the play moves toward its conclusion, is mesmerized by Sam. He admires Sam's faith when confronted with evidence capable of destroying faith. He wishes he could emulate Sam's piety and trust. But as it becomes increasingly clear that a mob is about to break into the inn, lusting for blood, Mendel, like the other minstrels, turns to Sam for help: surely he can save them; he must be one of the thirty-six just men God has placed on earth—or at least a miracle worker, or a mystical dreamer, but clearly someone with influence in high places. Sam, of course, encourages these protestations of devotion, and not until the final words are spoken do we discover how completely the other characters—and we—have been taken in.

Wiesel, as a Jew, could have had a polemical field day letting the priest represent the church and all Christians in their complicity with the pogroms. He is content, however, to sketch a priest who on the whole is ineffective rather than deliberately evil, one who even opens himself to danger on behalf of the Jews—when it is too late. On several occasions, sensing the growing ugly mood in the town, he urges the Jews in the inn to flee while there is still time, but the advice does not carry the requisite note of urgency.

Some of his concerns appear spurious, however, for while engaging in an intense exchange with Berish, he lets down his guard and reveals an ugly anti-Semitism that clearly lies close to the surface. In a sudden change of character he spews out invective: the Jews are indicted, God has forsaken them, they are no longer God's people, they deserve what they get. In a particularly searing exchange with Mendel, the priest declares that the Christians will be the judges of the Jews. To which Mendel responds:

> That you are God's whip, that is quite possible. But don't be so proud of it. God is closer to the Just struck by the whip than to the whip. God may punish the Just whom He loves, but despise the instrument of punishment; He throws it in the garbage, whereas the Just will find his way to the sanctuary.[6]

Mendel holds onto belief in a God of justice:

Between the man who suffers and the one who makes him suffer, whom do you think God prefers? Between those who kill in His name and those who die for Him, who, in your judgment, is closer to Him? (p. 98)

Even granting that the priest's intentions are sometimes honorable, he is weak when strength is called for, and equivocal when single-mindedness is essential.

On second thought, perhaps he is an appropriate symbol of a church that, in the face of evil done to others, and particularly to Jews, has often adopted timidity and equivocation as its official posture, let alone failing to rein in the mobs shouting "Christ–killers."

It is worth remarking, at this juncture, that although the playwright is a Jew, and all the characters, with the exception of Maria and the priest are Jews, *The Trial of God* is not a play for Jews only. Wiesel has often been asked why he writes so determinedly about Jews, rather than about universal humanity. His answer is convincing. When he writes about Jews, he *is* writing about all people, for the particularity of Jewishness is in reality a vehicle through which to explore what goes on in every human heart. Let the present writer testify: when I read Elie Wiesel, I learn not only about Jews but about myself, not only about Judaism but about Christianity. And I, too, am put on trial: Do *I* join the outraged cry of Berish that there is indeed a "case against God" to be explored, or do I remain silent? When I discover the fragility of Sam's "vindication" of God, do I accept the fact that I have used such arguments myself, or do I denounce them as unworthy? Indeed, confronted by the premature death of a single child, Jewish or no, do I acknowledge that it places the whole theistic enterprise in jeopardy? Or do I look for ways to bolster an already discredited defense?

Sam—we know nothing about Sam until the explosive Act III. His previous brief appearances, thanks to a handy spotlight, prepare us only to expect that he is going to be crucial to the plot line. Once on stage, he is not willing to reveal much about himself. Some of the others, however, are sure that they have seen him before. Indeed, whoever Sam is, his presence seems ubiquitous in places of evil, particularly in cities where there have recently been pogroms. Only Maria, as we have seen, is immune to his charms, and she has had to learn the hard way.

But however or wherever Sam appears, he is superb when he appears before a court of law. It is Sam who makes "the case for God," rebutting Berish point by point. We have heard such arguments before, and perhaps even made use of them ourselves.

Once the trial is underway and Berish has made a fiery opening statement of God's complicity in evil, Sam calmly replies that such anger and emotion prove nothing. There must be facts, data, information, otherwise there is no case at all.

Berish replies by offering facts aplenty. There were dwellings for one hundred Jewish families in Shamgorod, all destroyed. Houses of study were pillaged. Of the one hundred Jewish families who had inhabited Shamgorod, exactly two individuals survive—Berish and his daughter, Hanna, who is now insane as a result of the multiple rapes she suffered.

Sam feels no need to dispute such facts. Indeed, they can all be noted, but they provide no evidence against God. The only purpose they serve is to document certain terrible things that certain human beings did to certain others. But these are human deeds, not divine deeds. Sam smugly comments that, yes, men, women, and children were massacred, but "Why involve, why implicate their Father in Heaven?" (p. 128).

Very well, Berish will speak for the victims. But no, Sam counters, such "evidence" cannot be allowed either. Words from the lips of dead men are inadmissible in court. Does Berish have a pipeline to the dead? Did they give him permission to speak on their behalf? Surely, Sam responds, warming to the subject, it is more likely that if the dead are speaking at all, it is to thank that same Heavenly Father for removing them from the horrors of this world, and bringing them safely to the Heavenly Kingdom. What greater bliss could there be for humankind than immunity from the terrible things people—not God—do to one another?

And then, a strong argument from Sam: think of the Jews in times past who for centuries have been victims of pogroms and massacres, Crusades and Inquisitions. Did they renounce their faith in the face of such challenges? Did they not, on the contrary, reaffirm their faith, despite what happened, and continue to proclaim that whatever God does is right and just? Surely they have as much if not more cause to protest than Berish, and yet refuse to do so, taking their situations of extremity as occasions for praise, not complaint.

Sam emerges as the exemplary man of faith, whose trust is unshakable: "[God] may do with me whatever he wishes. Our task is to glorify Him, to praise Him, to love Him—in spite of ourselves." (p. 157)

We have left to the end the outcries of Berish, who is present throughout the play and has initiated the action. The omission has been deliberate, to avoid replicating at secondhand all the tensions and exchanges that mark the play at firsthand; and also to highlight, for more careful attention, the point in the trial where Berish seems to shift ground, as well as the crucial point that Sam fails to understand:

Before the trial, Berish has voiced a number of complaints, of which the following are only a few:

> To mention God's mercy in Shamgorod is an insult. Speak of his cruelty instead. (p. 43)

> I want to understand why He is giving strength to the killers and nothing but tears and the shame of helplessness to the victims. (p. 43)

> Let one killer kill for His glory, and He is guilty. Every man who suffers or causes suffering, every woman who is raped, every child who is tormented implicates Him. . . . Either he is responsible or He is not. If He is, then let's judge Him; if He is not, let him stop judging us. (p. 54)

What more natural than to hold a trial?

Toward the end, word comes that the mobs are approaching and that death is imminent. The priest makes another attempt to save his friends. Accept the protection of the cross (i.e., convert), while wearing Purim masks; later on, when the danger is over, the masks can be taken off, the conversions will be nullified, and they can "become Jewish again." (p. 155)

Berish, the accuser of God, does not waste time weighing this offer: "Well, the answer is no. My sons and my fathers perished without betraying their faith. I can do no less." (p. 154) Sam is astonished:

> I take note of the important fact that the prosecutor has opted for God against the enemy of God; he did so at the sacrifice of his life. Does it mean the case is to be dismissed? (p. 153)

But he has missed the point. Berish replies, "No, I have not opted for God. I'm against His enemies, that's all." (p. 156) The trial must go on:

> I live as a Jew, and it is as a Jew that I shall die—and it is as a Jew that, with my last breath, I shall shout my protest to God. And because the end is near, I shall shout louder! Because the end is near, I'll tell Him that He's more guilty than ever! (p. 156)

The power of this vigorous disclaimer is to be more fully appreciated in contrast to Sam's serene affirmation:

> I'm His servant. He created the world and me without asking for my opinion; He may do with both whatever He wishes. Our task is to glorify Him, to praise Him, to love him—in spite of ourselves. (p. 157)

Has Sam won the day? His affirmation does breathe piety and religious nobility, and there are times when we wish we could make it our own. But let us not, caught up in the rapidity of the closing exchanges, fail to hear what Berish is now affirming, and has been affirming throughout. His affirmation is strangely strengthened by the powerful negation on which it is built. That negation is a loud "no" to what is often called "consolatory theism." Never mind, the argument goes, however tough things are right now, some day the balance will be redressed, and the suffering within the interim will have been worth it. So when Mendel asks Sam, "What is there left for us to do?" Sam has a ready answer: "Endure. Accept. And say Amen." (p. 132)

Even angels can offer the message of consolation. In *Ani Maamin* (a cantata by Wiesel that *did* "work") the three Biblical patriarchs—Abraham, Isaac, and Jacob—go down to earth in the midst of the Holocaust and return to heaven to report what terrible things are going on. Abraham, the father of the faith, mounts an attack after the manner of Berish:

> What kind of Messiah
> Is a Messiah
> Who demands
> Six million dead
> Before He reveals Himself?

An angelic voice from heaven replies in words Sam could have spoken:

> God breaks
> And God consoles
> That is enough.

But Abraham is unpersuaded in the very depths of his being:

> No, it is not enough! . . .
> Never will the hearts
> Of my descendants
> Be consoled!

Isaac and Jacob support him: consolation is no answer. It heightens the problem rather than resolving it. It may have a place within the Jewish tradition, but one cannot remain passive in the face of evil.

So what shall we do? Rather than passivity, a dedicated aggressiveness is demanded. We are invited by another part of the Jewish tradition not to bury our concerns but to hold them up, to confront God with them, sometimes in anger. This is the manner of Jeremiah, who challenges God: "Why do the wicked prosper, and the treacherous all live at ease?" (Jer. 12:1)

We are permitted to question God, to challenge God, to demand an accounting from God. And this, rather than diminishing God is truly to take God seriously. As Wiesel has frequently remarked, "I do not have any answers, but I have some very good questions." The spirit of Berish remains alive and well.

On a whole other level of human existence, we find that the constraint to challenge God is also a vehicle for affirming God. Listen to Pedro, a man who has experienced unmentionable evil, crying out to his companion (in Wiesel's *The Town Beyond the Wall*):

> I want to blaspheme and I can't quite manage it. I go up against Him, I shake my fist, I froth with rage, but it's still a way of telling Him that He's there, that He exists, that He's never the same twice, that denial itself is an offering to His grandeur. The shout becomes a prayer in spite of me. [7]

The shouts of Berish are likewise a prayer in spite their anger.

One of Wiesel's teachers taught him that "Only the Jew knows that he may oppose God as long as he does so in defense of His creation."[8] The teacher taught his student well. All this and more is incorporated by Berish as he, too, refuses to be "consoled" by speech that smoothes things over.

Yes, he is a strange affirmer, this Berish. Loud, angry, audacious, single-minded—a Jew who refuses consolation and continues to defy to the very end. But a Jew, nevertheless, whose very accusation acknowledges the reality of the One accused, a Jew whose human words testify to an Eternal Word, a Jew who will die rather than renounce the tortured faith that remains his, despite all attempts by Sam or anyone else to dislodge it, a Jew whose "shout becomes a prayer," despite himself.

So in the end, Berish the innkeeper and the eminent scholars who held their own *din torah* in Auschwitz find themselves in the same position, except that the members of the court in Shamgorod were denied the chance to announce their verdict; the pogrom got there first.

Fifteen years before writing *The Trial of God*, Wiesel encapsulated the event in *The Gates of the Forest*. In that earlier book, a mere dozen lines are devoted to the trial at which God was found guilty as charged: guilty of murder.

But Gregor, the teller of the tale, indicates that his version of the story is not finished with the pronouncing of sentence. God still has the last word: the very next day, the three judges and all the witnesses in the trial were liquidated. Gregor sums up: "If their death has no meaning, then it's an insult, and if it does have a meaning, it's even more so."[9]

Years later, Gregor presses the question and elicits a variety of responses from a rebbe, who in the midst of deep perplexity is trying to identify avenues of affirmation. He reminds Gregor that the Hasidim can dance in fury as well as in joy, and can stand against God as a means of affirming God: "You don't want to dance," they say, addressing God, "too bad, we'll dance anyway."[10]

There is another mood as well, an insistence that the lacerating confrontation between God and humanity continue. The rebbe pours forth his anguish: "He's guilty; do you think I don't know it. . . . Yes, he is guilty. He has become the ally of evil, of death, of murder. . . ." The rebbe absorbs all the weight of the indictment and then goes on, transforming the declarations into a powerful interrogation: "The problem is still not solved. I ask you a question and dare you answer: *What is there left for us to do?*"[11]

What is there left for us to do? Only everything. What we cannot do is indict God and then excuse ourselves from enacting that justice whose absence first triggered our outrage. In his most audacious statement of human moral responsibility, Wiesel reminds us "that it is given to man to transform divine injustice into human justice and compassion."[12] There is an agenda for a lifetime.

At best, we can recognize that if there is an answer to Mendel's question—"And God in all this?"—it will be discerned only in an active response to the rebbe's question as well—"What is there left for us to do?"

Robert McAfee Brown
Professor Emeritus of Theology and Ethics
Pacific School of Religion
Berkeley, California

Notes

[1] Irving Abrahamson, ed., *Against Silence: The Voice and Vision of Elie Wiesel* (New York: Holocaust Publications, 1985), pp. 112–13.

[2] For further treatment of Purim and its meaning and celebration today, see Irving Greenberg, *The Jewish Way: Living the Holidays* (New York: Summit Books, 1988), pp. 224–57 ("Confronting Jewish Destiny: *Purim*").

[3] For further treatment by Wiesel of the book of Esther and its relation to Purim, see Elie Wiesel, *Sages and Dreamers: Biblical, Talmudic and Hasidic Portraits and Legends* (New York: Summit Books, 1992), pp. 133–51 ("Esther").

[4] David Blumenthal, *Facing the Abusing God: A Theology of Protest* (Louisville, Ky.: Westminster/John Knox Press, 1993, p. 250.

[5] Abrahamson, *Against Silence*, pp. 112–13.

[6] Elie Wiesel, *The Trial of God* (originally published by Random House, New York, 1979; first Schocken edition, 1986), p. 98. All subsequent page references for the play will be in parentheses at the end of each selection.

[7] Elie Wiesel, *The Town Beyond the Wall* (New York: Schocken Books, 1982), p. 123.

[8] Elie Wiesel, *A Jew Today* (New York: Vintage, 1979), p. 6.

[9] Elie Wiesel, *The Gates of the Forest* (New York: Schocken Books, 1982), p. 197.

[10] Wiesel, *The Gates of the Forest*, p. 198.

[11] Wiesel, *The Gates of the Forest*, p. 199 (emphasis added).

[12] Elie Wiesel, *Messengers of God* (New York: Summit Books, 1985), p. 235.

The Trial of God

CHARACTERS

MENDEL, the oldest, the wisest of them all. In his fifties. Tall, thin, majestic. A dreamer. He is the first minstrel. He knows how to look. And how to listen.

AVRÉMEL, the second minstrel. Melancholy, slightly ironical. A professional entertainer. He knows how to make others laugh, but he himself never laughs. In his forties.

YANKEL, the third minstrel. Noisy, at times coarse. A former coachman, he is restless. Mischievous.

BERISH, the innkeeper. Compared to the other three, he is a giant. Robust, angry. At the first provocation, he could split the table with his fists.

HANNA, his daughter. Mad? Absent. Humiliated, stained. Young, fragile.

MARIA, the servant. Thirty—or less. Tough. Plump but pretty. Outspoken, witty, aggressive.

PRIEST, Russian Orthodox. Short, heavyset, bon vivant. Kind but weak.

SAM, the STRANGER. Intelligent, cynical, extremely courteous. Diabolical. His age? Still young. Neat, almost elegant. Self-controlled.

All are dressed in the style of the seventeenth century. Boots and fur jackets: it is still cold outside. Maria has a black kerchief on her head; the men, fur hats. The priest wears a huge cross on his chest and the traditional robe.

THE SCENE

Somewhere in a lost village, buried in dust and darkness. The time: 1649, after a pogrom. Hate has won; death has triumphed. The rare survivors know that they are alone and abandoned.

An inn, at dusk. A large room with many spots left in darkness. A few tables, chairs. Candles. Empty bottles and glasses here and there. Shadows play threatening games on the walls.

Around a table, three Jewish minstrels order drinks. To forget? To free themselves from a distress that has no name? To celebrate the holiday of Purim whose miracles are told in the Book of Esther?

Purim: the annual day of fools, children and beggars. The carnival of masks. Everybody plays games, everybody gets drunk. Everybody wants to change.

The play should be performed as a tragic farce: a *Purimschpiel* within a *Purimschpiel.*

Its genesis: inside the kingdom of night, I witnessed a strange trial. Three rabbis—all erudite and pious men—decided one winter evening to indict God for allowing his children to be massacred. I remember: I was there, and I felt like crying. But there nobody cried.

Act One

As the curtain rises, MENDEL, AVRÉMEL *and* YANKEL *are sitting at a table.* MARIA *is wiping off the chairs at another.* BERISH *comes in, running; he is annoyed.*

BERISH

A glass, Maria. Hanna will get up any minute, and she'll be thirsty; and there is no glass in her room. I don't understand, Maria—do you? I have glasses everywhere, for everybody, except for Hanna!
  (*He goes to a table to pick up a clean glass*)

MARIA

You're running, running, Master. You're always running. Where to, Master? Where from? Why are you running? (BERISH *stops; he is startled*) Don't you see we've got customers? Hanna is asleep. Leave her alone. When she gets up, I will be there to take care of her, as I always do. But the customers, Master, have you forgotten them? Do I have to do everything, see everything, be everywhere?

BERISH

Be quiet, Maria. Hanna is restless. She'll get up any minute. She'll want her milk. Where have you put the clean glasses?

MARIA

In my pocket. In my bed . . . Don't you see I'm busy? Somebody has to clean up the place—right? (YANKEL *tries to catch their eyes*) You should pay more attention to the customers, Master.

3

BERISH

Don't tell me what to do. You're getting on my nerves. The customers are getting on my nerves. The whole world is getting on my nerves.

MARIA

Then you better get yourself another trade, Master. Better yet, get yourself another world.

BERISH

I'll get myself another helper if you don't stop this.

YANKEL

Leave her alone, innkeeper. Why don't you listen to us instead? We're waiting for you.

BERISH

Who are you?

YANKEL

His Majesty's special emissaries . . . Who do you think we are? Don't you have eyes? We are customers!

BERISH

What do you want?

YANKEL

Service.

BERISH

Service . . .

YANKEL

Does the word sound strange to you? We would like to order drinks.

BERISH

Drinks . . . (*He emerges from his daze*) All that people want is—drinks. (*He places a bottle and three glasses on their table*) One

4

of these days I'm going to close up this place, I promise you that. I'll sell it or burn it to the ground. And I'll get out of here.

MARIA

Right.

BERISH

You don't believe me? I'm telling you, I'll go away.

MARIA

You'll go away, you'll go away. . . . Where would you go?

BERISH

Anywhere. To the end of the world.

MARIA

No farther?

YANKEL
(*Laughs*)

Bravo, woman! Wouldn't you like to join us?

MARIA

Why—are you going to the end of the world too?

YANKEL

No, we have just come from there.

MARIA
(*To* BERISH)

Where *is* the end of the world?

BERISH

I don't know . . . Yes, I do. The end of the world is where you're not.

YANKEL
(*To* MARIA)
How do you manage to live under one roof with him?

MARIA
Mind your own business! He's my master. If he feels like insulting me, let him!

YANKEL
(*Mischievously*)
Wouldn't you like to join us?

AVRÉMEL
The end of the world . . . I remember it well. In my village there was a small dusty street. An old witch lived in the last shack. The children were convinced that it was the end of the world.

BERISH
The end of the world, the end of the world. In my home-town we were told . . . I forget what we were told.

MARIA
Forget it again, Master. You'll feel better.

AVRÉMEL
The witch and her shack. People would be seen entering it —no one was ever seen leaving it. The children were scared even to look at it—to look at it from far away.

MARIA
Can't you change the subject?

YANKEL
What's wrong with this one?

MARIA
Change the subject. And change the inn too. You're annoying us.

6

YANKEL

But we've said nothing. We would like to talk to you, innkeeper.

BERISH

I've got nothing to tell you.

YANKEL

How do you know?

AVRÉMEL

What if we asked you not to tell us anything but to listen to us while we tell you something?

BERISH

I'm not interested.

YANKEL

What do you mean, not interested? There must be something that interests you.

BERISH

Right! One thing: to see you get out.

YANKEL

All right, all right. We'll leave. Afterwards.

BERISH

After what?

YANKEL

Have you forgotten that it's Purim tonight? We must celebrate—have you forgotten how to celebrate?

MARIA

Change the subject, *please!*
    (YANKEL *looks at her quizzically*)

7

BERISH

Purim, Passover, Hannuka, it's all the same to me.

AVRÉMEL

Really? It's all the same to you? Then let us tell you. What does one do on Purim? One drinks. Especially when one is thirsty—and we are very thirsty, innkeeper.

YANKEL

Thirsty isn't the word for it.
(BERISH, *exasperated, is about to exit*)

AVRÉMEL

To keep a drink from someone who is thirsty—and on Purim eve, at that—is a sin, innkeeper, a terrible sin!

BERISH
(*Taken aback*)

A sin? Is that what you just said? You shouldn't have said it! Sin is a word I cannot bear to hear! You know why? Because of the sinner. You know who that is? Not I, not you, not even Maria—who knows something about it. It's . . . it's . . .

MARIA

Don't listen to him; he doesn't know what his mouth is saying. It happens to all of us. You are right, tonight is Purim —so we'll drink to that. (*To* BERISH) Do I give them another bottle?

BERISH

Give it to them—but get the money! Make them pay! Is that clear? (*Suddenly he freezes; he has heard* HANNA's *voice*) A glass, Maria! Quick! Give me a glass of milk, for heaven's sake! Move, woman! Move!
(*He exits hastily.* MARIA *places another bottle on the three minstrels' table*)

AVRÉMEL

A strange innkeeper, isn't he?

MARIA

So what! You have your problems, and he has his.

YANKEL

But he *is* strange, admit it. (MARIA *glares at him*) I am not
saying this to judge him. If he wants to be strange with his
customers, that's his problem—as you just said so eloquently
—but that doesn't make him less strange. And besides . . .

MARIA

Besides what? What else?

YANKEL

We could help him; it's our job, you know.

MARIA

Your job is to help strange people?

AVRÉMEL

Our job is to help people. (*Smiles*) Some become strange—
later.

MARIA
(*Less aggressively*)

Well, he is not like you or me. But then, who is? Sometimes
he keeps quiet for weeks on end; impossible to make him open
his mouth—not even to insult me. Then, all of a sudden and
without reason, he starts talking, shouting, quarreling: his
words just flow and flow—and nothing you do can stop him.
You mustn't hold it against him.

YANKEL

Oh, we don't. Why should we? We told you, we are not
here to judge him! Besides, we'd rather entertain him.

9

MARIA
(*Laughs*)
Entertain him? You must be joking.
(BERISH *reenters while the three Jews drink and sing a*
Purim tune)

BERISH
Not so loud!

YANKEL
We're barely whispering!

BERISH
You're whispering too loud!

YANKEL
Are we in a convent or in mourning? You want us to lament
when we are supposed to rejoice? No wonder we're the only
customers here; this place is for deaf-mutes with a sore throat.

BERISH
You talk too much.

YANKEL
You want us to stop talking? Nothing could be simpler.
(*To* AVRÉMEL) Right?

AVRÉMEL
Right. Pour us another glass. While we drink, we don't talk.

YANKEL
(*To* BERISH)
You are not much of a talker, are you. Is it that you, too,
would like another glass? Yes? Have one. It's on us.

BERISH
I'm not thirsty.

YANKEL

So what? Must one be thirsty to drink? Do birds fly only when they have someplace to go? They fly because they love freedom and the blue sky. We drink the way they fly.

AVRÉMEL

Listen—do you need reasons? There are reasons. Many reasons. You drink because Purim begins and Yom Kippur ends. Because you're in a good mood—or a bad mood. Because you won—or you lost. Because your daughter is getting married—or can't get married. A Jew who doesn't drink and doesn't know why he isn't drinking—something is wrong with his reasoning, believe me. For a Jew, a day without *yash* is like a love story without love.

MARIA
(*Somber, threatening*)

Did you say love?

AVRÉMEL

What's wrong with love?

MARIA
(*Imitates him*)

What's wrong, what's wrong . . . What isn't? Love was invented as an excuse for everything that goes wrong. You beat up someone and you say, "But it's because I *love* you." You cheat someone and again you say, "But it's because I *love* you." You mention the word love and everything is forgiven. Well, I do not forgive!

AVRÉMEL

A pity you feel that way about the subject.

MARIA

Why?

11

AVRÉMEL

Because we have got some good numbers on love in our repertoire.

BERISH

I'm not interested.

AVRÉMEL

One song? A shepherd boy singing of his love?

YANKEL

Just one? A shepherd girl dreaming that—

BERISH

I'm not interested.

AVRÉMEL

I guarantee you, you would enjoy it—you really would.

BERISH

I'm not interested, I tell you!

MARIA

How silly can you be! Grown-up men singing love songs about shepherd girls . . .

YANKEL

Why silly? Have you never been in love?

MARIA

Not with a shepherd boy! And I never sang! I am too busy.

AVRÉMEL

Too bad . . .

BERISH

Too bad . . . too bad . . . What do you mean: too bad? Never mind, don't tell me. Just drink up and be quiet!

(MENDEL *has been listening to this exchange, but seems*

remote, absorbed by his own thoughts. When he speaks, the whole mood changes abruptly)

MENDEL

Do you ever pray, innkeeper?

BERISH

Why do you ask? Why do you want to know? What business is it of yours whether I pray or not?

MENDEL

You don't sing, you don't drink, and often you don't talk —so I wanted to know what else you don't do.

BERISH

Well, no. I don't pray.

MENDEL

Don't you know how?

BERISH

I do, but I don't want to.

MENDEL

Any particular reason?

BERISH

That's my business!

MENDEL

Yours alone?

BERISH

Mine alone.

MENDEL

And God? (*Pause*) Where is God in all this, innkeeper?

BERISH
(*Fails to understand*)

God?

MENDEL

Don't you think it's His business as well? Don't you think
that whether you pray or not is also His concern?

BERISH
(*Angrily*)

Don't you think He can handle his own affairs? Do you
think He needs you to represent Him?

MARIA

I have seen customers fighting among themselves but never
with the master. Why don't you change the subject?

YANKEL

You are so wise, Maria. If King Solomon had had a sister,
you could have been her.

AVRÉMEL

We have a marvelous song about King Solomon and the
Queen of Sheba, would you like us to—

MARIA

Another love story? No, thank you.

YANKEL

Intelligent Maria. Clever Maria. You *are* clever. And careful. Men must be crazy about you.

AVRÉMEL

What a compliment! Doesn't that call for another bottle?

MARIA

Drinks cost money; compliments are free. You have got
money?

AVRÉMEL

Don't you trust us? (MARIA *shakes her head*) Poor woman. To live and not to have faith in man is sad, sad—and perhaps sadder than that. How can you love a man if you don't trust him? Answer my question!

MARIA

I have a better one for you: How are you going to pay for all these drinks? I'm warning you—we know how to take care of liars and cheaters and thieves. Don't think for a moment that you'll outsmart us! You won't!

YANKEL

Did I say King Solomon? I was wrong. I really meant Samson. (*He looks at her*) Yes, you remind me of Samson.
(MARIA *wants to reply, but* MENDEL *interrupts her*)

MENDEL

And God in all this, innkeeper? Tell me: Where is God in all this?

BERISH

What do you want from me? Am I His keeper? I resigned from membership in God—I resigned from God. Let Him look for another innkeeper, let Him find another people, let Him push around another Jew—I'm through with Him!

MARIA

Don't you worry, Master. You say things, but God isn't angry. How could He be? He isn't even listening.

YANKEL

Great, Maria! You know what's going on in heaven! Tell us! You're well informed! Are you God's confidante? Tell us! Tell us the truth: are you?

AVRÉMEL

Better yet, He is your confidant! He asks for your advice!

You tell Him what to do and when—and to whom! You even order Him around! Right?

YANKEL

Right! She is protecting her boss by ordering ours around.

AVRÉMEL

Why do you protect him? Why does he need protection? He is hiding things from us, isn't he?

MARIA

The devil with you and your questions!

YANKEL

He's got secrets, right? (*Pause*) So do we.

MARIA

Good for you. Keep them to yourselves.

YANKEL

Don't you want to know what they are? (MARIA *shakes her head*) And you, innkeeper? (BERISH *doesn't bother to acknowledge the question*) Not interested?

AVRÉMEL
(*To* YANKEL)

He thinks our secrets don't concern him. (*To* BERISH) They do, you know . . . You see, we drank your *yash,* we drank well —and we can*not* pay.
> (*He bursts out laughing, so does* YANKEL, *but not* MENDEL. BERISH *and* MARIA *look at each other. They're startled at first, but finally join the laughter*)

BERISH

Damn you, jokers! You win—I forgive you. You had your Purim game at my expense. Empty your glasses and go somewhere else. You've stolen enough from me.

MENDEL

Stolen from you? You think we're thieves?

BERISH

No. Just liars.

MENDEL

I protest.

BERISH

Go ahead, protest if you like . . . You show up under false pretenses, you fill your bellies with my drinks, without any intention of paying me . . . So what are you waiting for? Protest!

MENDEL

You misunderstand us, innkeeper. We *can* pay, although we have no money.

BERISH

How? Tell me how.

MENDEL

We'll play for you.

MARIA

There they go again with their love songs . . .

BERISH

You'll play? For me? Have I heard you right?

MENDEL

You haven't guessed, innkeeper? We are *Purimschpieler.* Why do you think we came here? To perform before the Jews of this community. They will pay; not you. For you we shall perform for nothing—in exchange for what you gave us. You see, you were wrong in suspecting us.

BERISH
(*Amazed*)

Beautiful! This is beautiful! And funny! (*He is seized with laughter*) Did you hear him? They came to perform! Here! For our Jewish community! (*Sits down*) Did you hear him, Maria? They came to perform a *Purimschpiel* for our Jews—here! Oh, it's funny—it's so terribly, terribly funny!

AVRÉMEL

What's so funny? We haven't begun performing yet, and he's laughing already!

YANKEL
(*To* MARIA)

Has *he* been drinking?
(MENDEL, *too, looks puzzled and questions* MARIA *silently*)

MARIA

Don't you know—don't you *know*—where you are? Is it possible that you don't know?
(*The three performers look at one another, puzzled.* BER-ISH *is still laughing—though now it is inwardly. A spot-light suddenly picks out the* STRANGER, *sitting in a dark corner of the room. He gives a quick smile, and the spot-light goes out*)

MENDEL

Tell us. (*Raises his voice*) I am ordering you to tell us.

MARIA

This is Shamgorod.

YANKEL
(*Freezes*)

No!

AVRÉMEL

You mean this is . . .

MENDEL

. . . two years ago. The gravediggers themselves were massacred.

AVRÉMEL

We are in Shamgorod . . . ?

MARIA

Near Shamgorod. And you came to play, for the Jews—

YANKEL

We didn't know . . .

MARIA

—the Jews of Shamgorod.

AVRÉMEL

We had no idea . . .

MARIA

That's why you came? To play? Here?

AVRÉMEL

How could we have guessed? We travel a lot—and most villages look alike. All the taverns, all the inns are the same . . .

YANKEL

This morning, as we approached, we thought: This looks like a nice, peaceful place; it must have a good Jewish population. We'll perform our *Purimschpiel* and make some money— enough to pay for a few hot meals and drinks.

(BERISH *laughs again noisily and stops abruptly*)

MARIA

So—you didn't know.

MENDEL

Sham-go-rod. (*Smiles sadly*) Well, well. We came to perform

a *Purimschpiel* in Shamgorod; it had to be Shamgorod!
> (*Now it is his turn to laugh but he cannot;* MENDEL's *inability to laugh is part of his tragedy*)

BERISH
(*Shakes himself*)
So—what are you waiting for? You came to perform? Perform! What are you good at? Well? Sing! Dance—stand on your head! You came to entertain the Jewish community of Shamgorod—so do it! The Jewish population of Shamgorod is waiting!

YANKEL
You are—

BERISH
What's the difference? I am the entire community—the entire population! The last Jewish father alive. Would you refuse the last Jewish father? Let me hear you sing—let me see you make funny faces!
> (BERISH *is excited, annoyed, outraged. He is torn between laughter and despair; he wavers as he seeks ways to avoid one or the other.* MARIA, *aware of his feelings, tries to prevent a catastrophe*)

MARIA
Go, good people, go. You made a mistake—now you know it. You drank and you didn't pay: forget it. Go. Take the road leading into the forest. (*She goes to the window and points*) Walk for an hour and a half or so. You'll find a river. Cross it, and you'll be in another village. There are still some Jewish families left there. Play for them.

BERISH
Yes—go! The sooner the better!

YANKEL
Tonight?

AVRÉMEL

Crossing the river may be dangerous. I cannot swim.

YANKEL

And I'm tired; my bones hurt. And I'm afraid of the forest.

MARIA

It's not too far. Go—you'll rest there.

AVRÉMEL

Can't we stay until tomorrow?

BERISH

No! (*Sarcastically*) Unless you agree to start the performance right away! Well? Go on! Get up! Start the play!

MENDEL
(*Softly*)

How can we? Without an audience?

BERISH

What about me? Am I nothing? And Maria—nothing? We
are nobody? Start!

MENDEL

We cannot, innkeeper. We are not in the mood.

BERISH

I am suddenly in the mood! For a *Purimschpiel!* Yes!

MARIA

Are you sure?

BERISH

Of course I am. Only . . . leave God out of it. You hear me?
I'm warning you!
> (*The three actors get up, put on their masks and move for-
> ward, and form a triangle, facing the audience. At a signal
> from* MENDEL, AVRÉMEL *begins*)

AVRÉMEL

What is life?
What is life?
A road
the child stumbles upon
in his dreams.
What is his dream?
What is his dream?
The hand
of an unknown
in the dark.
What is man?
What is man?
An empty road
for an empty dream.
An empty hand.
What is a drink?
Yes, what is a drink?
The song that fills the road,
and the dream;
the joy that moves the hand
and fills the heart
and gives man
what he never had.

THE THREE
(*pick up the refrain*)

What is a drink?
Yes, what is a drink?
The song that fills the road,
and the dream;
the joy that moves the hand
and fills the heart
and gives man
what he never had.

(*They bow, pull off the masks and start moving back to the table*)

MARIA

You *are* funny. Your joyous songs are sad—sad! I thought that Purim was a happy holiday!

AVRÉMEL

Well—it is!

MARIA

I wouldn't have guessed it—not from your performance! But then, you Jews love to do things upside down. You laugh when you're crying; you cry when you're laughing.

AVRÉMEL

But that's the meaning of Purim, Maria: a story in which everything is upside down. Do you want us to play it for you?

YANKEL

Say yes, woman. For once—say yes!

AVRÉMEL

It's a beautiful story, Maria. Haman plans to kill Jews, and God—

BERISH

Again? This house is off-limits to God, remember?

AVRÉMEL

May we at least recall the miracles?

BERISH

Yes, if you don't give Him credit.

YANKEL

So? Are we playing? I love stories in which Jews remain alive.

MARIA

I prefer your other holiday, Yom Kippur, when Jews can't eat—so I eat for all of them.

YANKEL

That's what *you* do on Yom Kippur? Then what do you do when it's *not* Yom Kippur? (*Pause. Grows moody*) But our Yom Kippur lasts all year round.

AVRÉMEL

Stop it, Yankel! Today is Purim! We must rejoice! We're *Purimschpieler!* We must fight sadness, not spread it!

YANKEL

I'm ready. What shall we play if not the story of Purim? How about the story of Joseph? The way he was sold as slave by his own brothers . . . We did it in Zhitomir, remember? People cried—oh, did they cry! They were *so* happy!

BERISH

No! I don't want to cry! And surely not over Joseph! I know all about him! You think I've forgotten his romance with Potiphar's wife? And you want me to weep over *his* tragedy?

YANKEL

Then, let's do the story of Esther.

BERISH

Out of the question! What's *that* story all about? A Jewish beauty who went to bed with an old king whose name is complicated—so complicated that I forgot it—sorry: so complicated that I never even knew it. And they were all there applauding her! Bravo, Esther! You did it! You made it! Now you are a princess! A queen! With an old senile husband who refuses you nothing. Why should I be happy for her?

AVRÉMEL

You're wrong, innkeeper. You insult everybody, but what

24

did Queen Esther do to you? Don't you like her? What don't you like about her?

BERISH

I don't like her story.

MENDEL

What's the matter, innkeeper? Don't you like women?

BERISH

Don't I like women? I love them more than you do! I even love your pretty queen! Let her come to me and you'll see: I'll make her happy. I guarantee it: she'll be happier with me than with her old fool of a husband.

MENDEL
(*Softly*)
And God in all this, innkeeper?

BERISH
(*Mimicking him*)
"And God in all this . . . and God in all this" . . . You're crazy, I swear you are! Can't you talk about anything else?

MENDEL

Do not make fun of God, innkeeper. Do not make fun of God—even if He is making fun of you.

BERISH

If? Did you say if?

MENDEL

It has not been proven yet.

BERISH

What else do you need—what more do you need—as proof? The pogrom of Shamgorod wasn't enough for you?

MENDEL

It was and is. More than enough.

BERISH

Then shout it!

MENDEL

I am a beggar. I have learned how to watch, to observe before uttering words that I may regret later. I have learned the art of waiting.

BERISH

I knew how to wait once . . . I waited and waited for redemption, and who do you think came? The redeemer? No: the killers.

MENDEL

And so you choose blasphemy. So be it. But is that an answer? If so, it means there is an answer. I am not sure there is . . .

BERISH

You're too complicated for me. I'm an innkeeper, not a rabbi!

MENDEL

You reject God—I do not. Why not? Because I am intrigued by Him. You see, Berish, I know man; I know what man is capable of. But God in all this?

BERISH

Why don't you ask instead: And Berish in all this? Let me answer you that one: God sought me out and God struck me down. So let Him stay away from me. His company is annoying me. He is unwelcome in my house. And in my life. If He wants to play, let Him play by Himself. If all this is a *Purim-schpiel*, let Him find himself another stage, another theater.

(MENDEL *and* BERISH *look at each other silently.* BERISH

wants to continue but does not: it is useless—God will not answer. BERISH *is tired; he has said too much*)

MENDEL
(*Smiles*)
I understand your anger, innkeeper. And I like it.

BERISH
Like it or not—who cares? Don't tell me that you share it.

MENDEL
I do not. But I like it anyway. It implies a question—

BERISH
A question? I asked no question!

MENDEL
You did. It is this: in our *Purimschpiel,* who is whose audience? Who is performing for whom?

AVRÉMEL
(*Clears his throat*)
I don't have a question—but I have an answer: Let us perform for you, innkeeper.
(*Again the three actors come forward and form a triangle*)

AVRÉMEL
(*sings*)

The falling leaves
fall for me;
the shining sun
shines for me;
the endless rivers
flow for me.
But I who live
for whom do I live?

27

THE THREE
But I who live
for whom do I live?

AVRÉMEL
The winter nights seem endless
endless for me
but—
(*He is interrupted by the* PRIEST, *who enters, bringing a cold breath of air inside*)

PRIEST
What weather, what weather!

MARIA
(*Sharply*)
Thanks for the information.

PRIEST
Nasty, nasty Maria . . . as always. Why are you so nasty?

MARIA
Why do certain people bring out the nastiness in me?

PRIEST
You inflame their senses, Maria. You incite them to do things they shouldn't even dream about. Why don't you come to confession?

MARIA
I'm scared.

PRIEST
Of what?

MARIA
Temptation. (*Pause*) Yours, Father.

PRIEST
(*Enjoys the joke*)

You can't be fooled, Maria, can you? It's not my fault: the flesh is weak, whereas the devil is not.

MARIA

The devil, the devil . . . You can't do without him; what would he do without you?

PRIEST

I prefer to think of what I could do with you.

MARIA

I see myself as you see me . . . disgusting.

PRIEST

Never mind, Maria, I forgive you—God forgives you. We forgive you the sins we could commit together—if only you would be agreeable.

MARIA

Are you talking about sin or punishment?
(*She leaves him in haste to pour herself a glass of water and him a glass of wine. The* PRIEST *turns his attention to the three Jews and* BERISH, *who, having been interrupted, observe him with an expression of slight annoyance on their faces*)

PRIEST

What are *you* doing here? I haven't seen new Jewish faces here for quite some time.

MENDEL

We are beggars and wandering minstrels.

PRIEST

So you are celebrating tonight? At whose expense?

MENDEL

We are celebrating a Jewish holiday: Purim.

PRIEST

Oh yes, I remember. You are happy because Haman, the great patriot and brave prime minister, was hanged. If you could hang all Christian patriots, that would really be a cause for celebration, right?

MENDEL

Haman was not Christian—if our recollections are correct.

PRIEST

Don't tell me he was Jewish . . . Poor man, how you hated him!

MENDEL

Again—if our recollections are correct—he hated us; he planned to kill us all.

PRIEST

Naturally! What else did you expect? You plotted against him all the time, you had one of your girls seduce his king, so he had to defend himself, didn't he? But you got him in the end, didn't you? You are shrewd; oh yes, Jews always have been. Shrewd and lucky. So you got your man—poor Haman —and nailed him to his cross.

AVRÉMEL

To his what?!

PRIEST

You heard me. Why play the innocent now? Don't you know that Jews killed all their opponents, and always in the same manner. You hate everybody—and then you wonder why you are hated.

MENDEL

We do not hate anybody.

PRIEST

Impossible. It wouldn't be natural. How could you not answer hate with hate?

MENDEL

We could—we can.

PRIEST

Impossible. In your place, I would hate the whole world. I would hate heaven and earth. How can you not hate them?

MENDEL

We can.

PRIEST

God doesn't love you, admit it. Tell me: Why doesn't God love you?

MENDEL

I don't know.

MARIA

Neither do you.

PRIEST

Are you taking their side, daughter? You'll burn in hell.

MARIA

Better in hell with them than in paradise with you.

PRIEST

I knew you were nasty, Maria, but not that you were foolish as well. This is the wrong time to show your love for Jews. Things are happening. Shamgorod is agitated because of what occurred in Miropol. A Kotasky child died, and people speak of Jewish malediction and the evil eye. No, daughter, this is not the time for a good Christian to be interested in Jews.

BERISH

Are they starting all over again? Will there never be an end to hate?

PRIEST

As long as there are Jews, they will inspire hate.

BERISH

But except for myself and my daughter, there are no Jews left here!

PRIEST

They can be found elsewhere. In other cities, other villages. Leave it to their enemies; they'll find some to hate. To kill.

BERISH

It's madness, madness!

PRIEST

True, Berish. It is madness and we are helpless. It will disappear when you do, not before.

MENDEL

It will never disappear—not even when the victims are all gone. What would you do if you had no Jews to hate, to vilify, to murder? You don't know? I do. You would begin hating, despising, killing one another. You learn, you practice on us; later you will do it to your own, and then to yourself.

PRIEST

You speak well and without fear. Who are you?

MENDEL

A Jew.

PRIEST

What kind of Jew?

MENDEL

Is there more than one kind? In your eyes, all Jews are alike.

PRIEST

You speak without fear—I want to know why.

MENDEL

Beggars learn fast how to vanquish fear.

PRIEST
(*Looks at each of the three*)
I hope this holds true—especially tonight.

BERISH

Why tonight?

MENDEL

I think I understand. (*To the* PRIEST) How bad is it? Be frank with us, please.

PRIEST
(*Bites his lip; then with concern*)
I came here to see you, Berish. I didn't know you had company. I came to warn you. And give you some friendly advice. Go away for a few days, a few weeks. Hide somewhere . . . in the forest perhaps. With friends. Anywhere. Go underground until—until it's over. People are thirsty for Jewish blood, that's all I can tell you . . . (*Takes hold of himself; his expression changes again*) And I am thirsty for some good wine or *yash*. Well, Maria?
(MARIA *serves him.* BERISH *moves closer to the* PRIEST.)

BERISH

Are you serious? Or is it simply your way of scaring us— and getting something in return? Why did you come?

PRIEST

Christian charity, Berish. Pure Christian charity. It still exists, you know. We have known each other for years. I

33

want to help you. Protect you—and your daughter. Can you go away? Stay with a Christian family? I would gladly take you into my home, but it isn't safe: people know of our friendship. How about going to Zhitomir? To Berditchev perhaps?

> BERISH

When?

> PRIEST

Soon . . . if not sooner. Tomorrow? Tonight? If not . . . if things get bad . . . really bad—we can always use my method.

> BERISH

What do you have in mind?

> PRIEST

You know, the cross . . .

> BERISH

Thank you for that kind of protection!

> PRIEST

Do you know one that is more efficient—and less costly?

> BERISH

It's like the Angel of Death offering to safeguard the living.

> PRIEST

Thank you for the analogy. But then, the Angel of Death has at least one virtue—he is reliable. One can count on him. On whom can you count?
>
> (BERISH *does not reply*)

> MARIA
> (*Replies for him*)

God.

34

PRIEST

God?

MARIA

Yes, God. Theirs. Yes—they, too, have a God of their own.
I have faith in Him.

PRIEST

Why shouldn't you, Maria? You are not Jewish. You may
trust the God of the Jews; not they. (*Puts his arm on* BERISH's
shoulder) But you may trust me, innkeeper. I am your friend.
(*To the three Jews*) You, too, I am on your side. Listen to me.
Go away. Right now. And don't say I haven't warned you.
(*The* PRIEST *exits.* MARIA *closes the door behind him*)

MARIA

Don't pay any attention, Master. He's drunk.

BERISH

(*Paces up and down the room*)
I'll kill, Maria. I swear it to you. I swear, this time I'll kill.

MARIA

I could take Hanna.

BERISH

And go where?

MARIA

To Zapritza. My mother's hut is large enough for Hanna
and myself.

BERISH

She stays with me.

MARIA

You come too.

35

BERISH
And they?

MARIA
We could *all* go there.

BERISH
They know about your mother. They would find us in no time.

MARIA
Anyway, we are foolish to pay attention to a drunkard's rambling.

YANKEL
(*Wanting to be reassured*)
Eh, he tried to scare us.

AVRÉMEL
And succeeded very well.

BERISH
(*Still following his vision of horror*)
This time I'll kill, I swear to you, this time I'll kill.

MENDEL
No. (*All look at him, puzzled*) I don't mean you, Berish. Not you alone. I mean all of you. All of us. I said: No. No to fear. What! A few words are enough to stifle our song? Tonight is Purim, and Purim commemorates the end of fear and the beginning of joy.

BERISH
You're a mad, crazy beggar. You're mad.

MARIA
The old man is right! What about—

BERISH

Maria! Are you, too, losing your mind?

MENDEL

Do you have a better solution, innkeeper? No? Then try ours. Let us proceed. As though the priest had not come. As though there had not been a pogrom in Shamgorod. As though killers had no license to kill. Let us celebrate Purim as our ancestors did.

BERISH

You are mad, crazy beggars. (*Pause*) We are all mad. Purim is over. For good.

MENDEL

So what! Only madmen know how to pay tribute to Purim! Purim is for madmen!

MARIA

Long live madness! Long live Purim! Come, I'm pouring drinks! For everybody, myself included!
(*They drink; MARIA serves them*)

YANKEL

Eh, Maria! Are you in love?

MARIA
(*Nastily*)

Is that how you imagine a woman in love? You lack imagination, my poor little minstrel.

AVRÉMEL

How is it to be in love, Maria? What does one feel?

YANKEL

Come, tell us!

MARIA

I'm in a good mood. Why do you want to spoil it? Tonight

I want to celebrate with you; tonight I want to forget that I ever was in love—please, friends, leave me alone.
(*They all laugh*)

MENDEL

We have drunk. We have sung. We haven't performed yet. Let's show our gracious host what good actors we really are. What shall we play?

BERISH

Can I choose?

MENDEL

Of course; it's your theater.

MARIA

Long live theater . . . What's theater?

BERISH

When you do something without doing it, when you say something without saying it, while thinking that you did say, and you did do something—anything—that's theater.

MARIA

So—I have made theater! Bravo myself!

AVRÉMEL

What play should we put on?

YANKEL

I've an idea: The unknown master who suffers from being too well known.

AVRÉMEL
(*Shakes his head*)

Too unrealistic.

YANKEL

Then King Solomon and the devil who seized his throne.

AVRÉMEL

Too realistic.

YANKEL

How about—in spite of our host's objections—the story of
Esther? It enables you to drink. A lot . . . Without God, that's
a promise!

MARIA

Good! I'll be the queen.

YANKEL

But you're not Jewish!

MARIA

Nor am I a queen. But who will play the queen? You
perhaps?

YANKEL

Hey, innkeeper, don't you have a daughter?

MARIA

She's a queen, all right, but don't count on her.

AVRÉMEL

I refuse to worship a Jewish queen who is not Jewish!

YANKEL

Then let's play something else. The sacrifice of Isaac? It's
good— It makes you cry!

BERISH

Not me.

YANKEL

Are you against Isaac too? What did *he* do to you?

BERISH

I distrust miracles. They exist only in books, and books say anything.

AVRÉMEL

So do you, innkeeper. You say things . . . Don't you know that certain things may not be said aloud? When I was my community's official jester, I occasionally offended a dignitary, and could, as a direct result, neither eat nor talk except standing. Do you think that God is more indulgent than local dignitaries?

YANKEL

True, how true. *You* could easily be the cause of our misfortunes. You talk, you talk, and suddenly there is a disaster at the door—and it's because you've talked.

MARIA

And the show? And the theater? What's happening to our celebration?

MENDEL
(*Meditating*)

Berish . . . do you know the priest?

BERISH

Eh . . . yes.

MENDEL

Do you know him well?

BERISH

Yes . . . I think so. I know him as one knows a neighbor, a customer—as one knows . . . someone one knows.

MENDEL

What do you think of him?

BERISH

As priest?

MENDEL

As a person.

BERISH

Greedy, wicked like the others. No, it's not true. He is not like the others. Not too brave but not at all wicked.

MENDEL

Should we take him seriously?

BERISH

His sermons?

MENDEL

His warnings.

BERISH
(*Hesitates*)

He drinks a bit, but . . . pogroms should always be taken seriously.

MENDEL

Then a pogrom is possible?

BERISH

A pogrom is always possible.

MENDEL

In Shamgorod? Against whom?

BERISH

Don't you know them? They don't need Jews to unleash a pogrom against Jews.

MENDEL

Maria?

MARIA

I agree. It's possible. Especially since the events took place
. . . The rebellion has driven everybody mad . . . The Ukraini-
ans are angry with the Poles but it is the Jews they're killing
. . . A few words, a few bottles, and the whole village is on
fire. But . . .

MENDEL

But?

MARIA

He is often drunk. He must have remembered the last
pogrom, so he—

YANKEL

Perhaps God will have mercy on us.

BERISH

Starting again?

AVRÉMEL

You don't like it? Don't listen. We need God's mercy—why
not ask for it?

YANKEL

Why not beg for it?

BERISH

Because God is merciless, don't you know that? How long
will you remain His blind slaves? I no longer rely on Him; I'd
rather rely on the drunkenness of the priest. (*Sees the shock on
their faces*) What is it? You don't like the way I speak? How
do you expect me to speak unless you want me to lie? God is
God, and I am only an innkeeper. But He will not prevent me
from letting my anger explode! He will not succeed in stifling
my truth—and neither will you!

MENDEL

What *is* your truth?

BERISH

I don't know what it is, but I know that it is an angry truth! Yes, I am boiling with anger! Don't ask me why, you know why! If you don't, I do! But you do know why. You are in Shamgorod, you must know. To mention God's mercy in Shamgorod is an insult. Speak of His cruelty instead. You see what I mean?

MENDEL

I see. Continue.

BERISH

I want to understand why He is giving strength to the killers and nothing but tears and the shame of helplessness to the victims.

MENDEL

So—you don't understand. Neither do I. Is that enough reason to reject Him? Suppose you understood, would you accept?

BERISH

No, I would not.

MENDEL

Why not?

BERISH

Because I would refuse to understand—I would refuse to understand so as not to forgive Him.

MENDEL

Because you have suffered?

BERISH

My suffering has nothing to do with it.

MENDEL

Whose then?

BERISH

Whose? (*Changes his tone*) Never mind.

MENDEL

Now *I* want to understand.

BERISH

You won't. Nobody ever will . . .
(*A mood of sadness sets in. Everyone remembers his own experiences*)

MARIA

On my life, I swear on my life, good people, that my master is telling the truth. You will never understand what took place here. What we have seen, nobody should ever be forced to see.

MENDEL

I want to know. (MARIA *shakes her head*) I insist. (*With anger*) I want to know.

BERISH

Look at him! An angry comedian! Since when are *you* angry?

MENDEL
(*Hesitates*)

I don't know . . . No, I do know. It happened in another life. Before I became a minstrel. Before I became a beggar.

BERISH

I was an innkeeper; I still am. And yet I have the impression that since that night I am no longer the same person. That night, life stopped flowing. Nothing matters any more. Nothing exists. Berish is alive, but I am not him. Life goes on, but outside me, away from me.

MENDEL

But life does go on. Isn't that a reason to rejoice? Life continues as before . . .

BERISH

Not as before . . . Before, it was different—I was different. The sap of the earth enriched my own; the blood of the world flowed in my veins. I loved my steady, faithful customers. Occasionally, one or the other—one and the other—misbehaved or refused to pay. Well, my fists were strong enough to teach them a lesson. I was happy and I liked seeing happiness around me. No one left my home or this inn empty-handed. Or with an empty stomach. I loved to give. Why not? I took from the rich and gave to the poor. To glimpse even a fleeting smile on a sad face was for me the most beautiful reward: I had to make an effort to contain my foolish tears. And God in all this? You want to hear the truth? It happened that He would touch me, on the shoulder, as if to remind me: See, Berish—I exist—I, too, exist! Then I would give Him something just to make Him happy: a little prayer for the Sabbath, an act of contrition for Yom Kippur, a good meal for Passover eve. And so, both of us satisfied, we would then go on with our separate daily routines. It's stupid but I can't help it: before, I hardly thought of Him; now I do—and I hate myself for it!

YANKEL

Me—before? I would let the horses gallop away, and I would shout into the wind: I am coming, God of my slain fathers, I am coming to offer you my services. Where do you want me to take you?

AVRÉMEL

I was singing, singing about anything and everything under the sun, and even above—and so was He . . . And we tried to outdo one another.

(They reminisce nostalgically—except for MENDEL, *who prefers not to reveal himself)*

45

MENDEL

And you, Maria?

MARIA

Me? Before your before, I had my own. I discovered love
and the cruelty of love . . . I didn't know that . . . But what
am I doing? Why am I blabbering silly things? You speak of
God, and I— Sometimes, at church, I hear the priest describe
our Lord's suffering—and I wonder whether the Lord isn't
suffering because He must listen to sermons! (*She has an idea*)
Why not accept—or at least consider—his proposal?

BERISH
(*Startled*)

What proposal?

MARIA

The priest's.

BERISH

And go into hiding? You know it would be useless.

MARIA

No, I mean . . . his offer of protection. What would it cost
you? Why not play it safe?

MENDEL

And kneel before the cross?

MARIA

Who would see you? Who would know? You do it one-two-
three and it's over. Do it. Do it for your God or mine. You
know what? Do it for me. To make me feel better.

BERISH

Maria, Maria—why do you talk such nonsense? Would you
want to see us betray our faith?

46

MARIA

I want to see you alive—do you hear me? Alive!

BERISH

You want us to live a lie?

MARIA

Life is not a lie—to live is not a lie! What does it cost you to pay a silly price for something that is priceless? To bend a little bit and say a few words while thinking about other things? What does it cost you to say a few nice words to my God while silently praying to yours? Your God will forgive you, I promise you.

MENDEL

Perhaps He will. I will not.

MARIA

I knew it, old man! You are going to give us trouble! Why did you come here? Why are you harsher than He? Where is it written that you must die for God? I'm nothing but a simple peasant woman, I don't know how to read or write. But I know—yes, I *know*—that life is given by God, I *know* that it is precious and unique just as God is. God is God: sometimes He is kind, other times He is not—He's still God! The same is true of life: sometimes it is sweet, other times it is not—but life is life and it justifies everything.

BERISH

No, Maria! There are certain things it does not justify.

MARIA

But why, Master? Why? Why make a big thing out of nothing?

MENDEL

To die is nothing?

MARIA
(*Impatiently*)
I'm not speaking about death; I'm speaking about God.

MENDEL
And God is nothing?

MARIA
Don't confuse me—I'm confused already! I didn't say that
God is nothing; on the contrary: He's too much! My God does
not persecute me. Yours does nothing else. Why not play a
trick on Him? Why not turn your back on Him for a day or
a week? Just to teach Him a lesson!

MENDEL
What lesson? That we can go down on our knees?

MARIA
So what! You're on your knees—whisper a few quick sentences—and one-two-three, you're back on your feet!

MENDEL
Wrong, Maria. Once you're on your knees, you can't stand
up straight again.

MARIA
(*Almost hysterically*)
Then make believe! For God's sake, make believe!

MENDEL
That's playing games, Maria! We don't play *such* games!

MARIA
(*Desperately*)
And . . . Hanna? Little Hanna, Master? What about Hanna?
(*A white quasi-transparent silhouette appears at the door.
Frail, she seems to walk on air. They all perceive her presence
at the same time*)

BERISH

Hanna! What are you—

HANNA

Voices—I heard voices. I love to hear voices.

MENDEL

(*With tenderness*)

What do they say?

HANNA

They say that love is possible. And pleasant. That happiness
is God's gift to all of his children. They tell me: "Dance." And
I dance. They tell me: "Sing." And I dance and I sing. They
tell me: "Love." And I love—I love everybody. They tell me:
"Live." And I say: "But I *am* alive. Can't you see I am alive?"

MARIA

Come, little girl. Let's go back to sleep.

HANNA

I'd rather stay. You have guests. Do I know them?

MENDEL

No, Hanna. I don't think so.

HANNA

I would like to make your acquaintance, believe me. I am
not afraid, I am really not afraid of strangers.

MENDEL

We believe every word.

HANNA

Why should I be afraid? No one has hurt me. Winter nights
are quiet here. If some stars are soaked with blood, it is because the sun has penetrated the dark sweet body. Night is
screaming, and its screams become stars, don't you see? But

that has nothing to do with us, so why should I be afraid of Night? And—

MARIA

You're absolutely right, little girl. There is nothing to be afraid of. And nobody is afraid of anything. Come, let's go to your room.

HANNA

But it isn't polite to leave guests just like that! Please, Maria! (*To* MENDEL) Who are you?

MENDEL

Friends.

HANNA

My father's friends?

MENDEL

Yours too.

BERISH

They're *Purimschpieler.*

HANNA

Really? Oh, I'm so happy. Please, play for me. Sing something—anything! A lullaby? A fairy tale?

YANKEL
(*To* AVRÉMEL)

Well? Go on, sing!

AVRÉMEL

You know the song of the young girl who dreamed and dreamed and never stopped dreaming? Years and years went by and she was still dreaming . . .

HANNA

Oh, I love it! Go on, please!

AVRÉMEL

One night she met a beggar who smiled at her sadly. "I am sorry," said the little girl. "I cannot offer you anything, since I don't own anything; I own nothing, since all this is a dream, only a dream." "It doesn't matter," said the beggar. "I want nothing from you except . . ." "Except what?" asked the little girl. And the beggar answered, "Take me into your dream." And then she awoke.

HANNA

Oh, how beautiful! (*Lowers her voice*) Am I the little girl? Are you in my dream? Am I going to wake up? Will I discover that the beggar has vanished? And you too? (*Laughs*) Do not worry, friends. You will never vanish: I hereby proclaim you immortal!

(*They are all silent and motionless for a moment*)

MARIA

Come, dear. Come with me. You will see our friends again. Tomorrow.

(*The two women exeunt slowly*)

MENDEL
(*Sighs*)

Tomorrow.

(*The silence is heavy*)

YANKEL

I don't know—when I think of tomorrow I remember yesterday. A village, not far from Nemirov. I remember the corpses in the streets and in the courtyards. I remember being told to put them in my carriage and go from nowhere to nowhere. I remember talking to my horse in order not to lose my mind. I remember talking to them as I am talking to myself. And I'm telling them, I'm telling them . . .

AVRÉMEL

The last wedding. The last tune. The last riddle. The guests laugh and weep at the same time. I watch the groom and the bride, I thank heaven for bringing them together. Suddenly —the killers arrive and there is blood everywhere. Everything happens so fast that instinctively I continue to make rhymes; it takes me a long while before I realize that I am trying to entertain the dead.

BERISH

I remember . . . (*Takes hold of himself*) No, I won't tell you what I remember.

YANKEL

Afraid. I remember being afraid. Afraid to go back on the road with another carriage, another horse.

AVRÉMEL

As for me, I was afraid to sing for the dead. Afraid that I could and afraid that I could not . . .

BERISH
(*To* MENDEL)

And you? Aren't you afraid?

MENDEL

Not at all.

BERISH

I don't believe you. You *are*; we all are.

MENDEL

I have seen the limits of truth and the boundaries of man; I have seen farther and looked higher—fear no longer has a hold over me.

BERISH

I don't believe you.

MENDEL

I have looked death in the eyes; I have seen God at work.
And I have never turned away.

BERISH

Everybody is afraid. Afraid of suffering or of witnessing
suffering. Afraid of death or of witnessing death.

MENDEL.

I am not afraid.

BERISH

Everybody trembles, and you're no exception. The whole
world frightens *me*. Strangers and neighbors, men who are too
drunk or too lucid, too passionate or too indifferent, they all
frighten me. Everything does. Sunshine and darkness. Dawn
and dusk. Streets and cellars. Forests and fields. Clouds and
rainbows. They all help the enemy. Don't protest—you think
as I do. You are also afraid.

MENDEL

I am not afraid.

BERISH

You're lying, you're a liar.

MENDEL

Not I, innkeeper. Not I.

BERISH

"And God in all this?" Have you no fear of God—not even
of God?

MENDEL
(*Hesitates*)
What if I told you that I fear *for* God? You seem to confuse
fear and awe. I am in awe of God, but I do not fear Him.

53

BERISH

I don't believe you. When the whole world is our enemy, when God Himself is on the side of the enemy—when God *is* the enemy, how can one not be afraid? Admit it: you do fear Him. You neither love nor worship Him. All He evokes in you is fear.

MENDEL

Man steals and kills, but it is God you fear?

BERISH

Men and women are being beaten, tortured and killed— how can one *not* be afraid of Him? True, they are victims of men. But the killers kill in His name. Not all? True, but numbers are unimportant. Let one killer kill for His glory, and He is guilty. Every man who suffers or causes suffering, every woman who is raped, every child who is tormented implicates Him. What, you need more? A hundred or a thousand? Listen: either He is responsible or He is not. If He is, let's judge Him; if He is not, let Him stop judging us.
(*The dispute has made them all angry.* MARIA *has returned. She has been listening*)

MARIA

Have you all gone mad? For God's sake, Master, stop talking about God!

MENDEL

We wouldn't mind, Maria. If only He left *us* alone.

BERISH

Right. We shall not let go of Him! (*To the minstrels*) You wanted to put on a play? Do it! But I want to choose the subject. I want a *Din-Toïre!* That's what I want!

MARIA

What's that?

54

YANKEL

That's new; we've never played that.

AVRÉMEL

A *Din-Toïre?* Just like that? On what grounds? Called by whom?

MARIA
(*Annoyed*)

What is it?

YANKEL

A *Din-Toïre* with whom? Against whom?

BERISH

You want to perform in honor of Purim? Good, let's stage a trial! Against whom? Imbeciles, haven't you understood yet? Against the Master of the universe! Against the Supreme Judge! That is the spectacle you shall stage tonight. It is that or nothing. Choose!

MENDEL

You mean a real . . . fake trial?

BERISH

Absolutely!

MENDEL

With God—blessed be His name—as . . . defendant?

BERISH

A trial like any other, except that this time, yes. Yes! With Him as defendant.

YANKEL

And what if the verdict is—

AVRÉMEL

—guilty?

BERISH

So what! It's Purim—on Purim, everything goes! (*Triumphantly*) Well? You agree?

55

(A long silence follows. YANKEL *and* AVRÉMEL *show their reluctance. Not* MENDEL*)*

BERISH
(Excited)

You agree? Do you?! You have the courage to do my kind of *Purimschpiel?* Tell me! And go to the end of things—and utter words no one has ever uttered before? And ask questions no one has ever dared ask before? And give answers no one has ever had the courage to articulate before? And to accuse the *real* accused? Do you have that kind of courage? Tell me!

MENDEL
(Looks at him intently)

Yes, innkeeper. *(His two friends scrutinize him, startled)* Yes, tonight is Purim, and tomorrow we may be dead. The priest may be right—or wrong; the enemy may win or wait. Let's stage your play, innkeeper. And stage it as free men.

YANKEL

Free to begin—

AVRÉMEL

—and free to conclude?

BERISH
(Jumps up, shouts)

Bravo, my friends! Listen, world! Hear us, mankind! There is going to be a trial!

MENDEL

Tonight we will be free to say everything. To command, to imagine everything—even our impossible victory.

(The spotlight again picks out the STRANGER. *The three wanderers seem to have aged. Only* BERISH *is ecstatic.* MARIA *shakes her head)*

CURTAIN

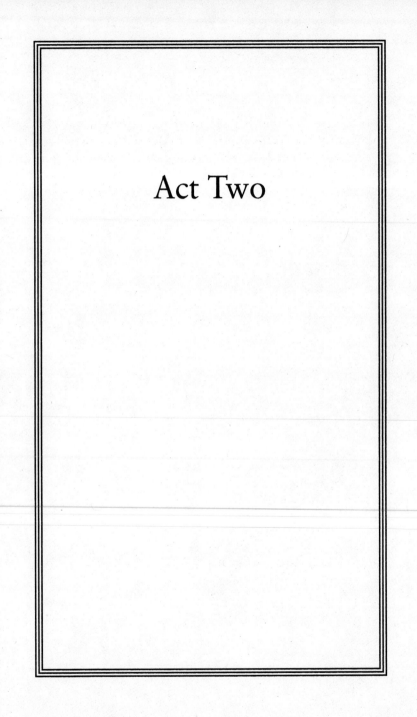

Act Two

The tables and benches have been rearranged to give the impression of a tribunal. The characters perform less than before, now that they are consciously performing specific parts.

YANKEL

I want to have a good time. And wear my mask.

AVRÉMEL

In the courtroom?

YANKEL

Tonight is Purim, yes or no? It's Purim everywhere, yes or no? Can you imagine Purim without masks? I cannot. When I was a coachman, even my poor horse wore a mask on Purim.

AVRÉMEL

But who told you this is the way to celebrate Purim? Your horse?

YANKEL

Please, do not make fun of my horse! My horse brought martyrs to the cemetery! I am not a scholar, I'm a coachman. I taught myself the things I know. And I'm telling you: a Purim without masks is a Purim I don't like.

AVRÉMEL

But we are having a trial!

YANKEL

Let's have it with masks! I love Purim masks!

AVRÉMEL

Because they hide the visible—or the invisible?

YANKEL

Because they are amusing!

AVRÉMEL

What about dignity, Yankel?

YANKEL

What about it? Coachmen have no lessons to learn from jesters!

AVRÉMEL

Don't get angry!

YANKEL

Then stop giving me sermons! I don't like them! You're a judge, I'm a judge: we're equal before . . . before the defendant!

AVRÉMEL

But you don't behave like a judge—you behave like a clown!

MARIA

Oh, I love clowns.

AVRÉMEL

What are we playing tonight: clowns or judges?

YANKEL

What's the difference *what* we play? What's important is that we *play*. And I cannot play if I don't wear a mask!

AVRÉMEL

All right, all right! Put it on! Quickly! Go! (YANKEL *obeys*)
If I were to see you in the coachman's seat, I would wonder
who was the coachman and who the horse.

YANKEL

Insulting me again?

AVREMEL

Don't behave as if we were at the market! Please!

YANKEL

What's wrong with being at the market? Why do you make
fun of those who go there? I used to go there often. I loved
it. The sounds, the shouting, the smell. Sometimes I brought
happy people there who returned home unhappy, or the other
way around, simply because they looked where they shouldn't
have. I prefer the market place to the synagogue any day!

AVRÉMEL

Once a coachman, always a coachman.

YANKEL

Now he's against coachmen! Ah, what have we done to
you? Have we stolen your money? Your daughter perhaps?

MARIA
(*To* MENDEL)

Are they playing? (*To the two men*) I, too, like the market
better than the church.

YANKEL

How about coachmen? How do you feel about coachmen,
Maria?

MARIA

Men! (*Spits*) They're all alike! I hate men!

MENDEL
(*Authoritatively*)

Enough! (*Pause*) Enough, I said!

YANKEL

Why? Am I not free? You said it yourself: tonight we're all free! Let me do and say what I please! Let me be free tonight.

MENDEL

We are free to play our parts of free men, but not free to act like clowns, Yankel.

YANKEL

Don't clowns have a right to be free?

MENDEL

They do, as clowns. But tonight we are judges. We will speak on behalf of the entire community.

AVRÉMEL

The entire community? What community? There is none in Shamgorod, remember?

MENDEL

Whenever one of us speaks, he speaks for all of us. Even when he is alone, a Jew represents more than himself—he represents a Jewish community, if not the Jewish community.

AVREMEL
(*Pointing at* YANKEL)

That's too complicated for him!

YANKEL

Community, community, I happen to love that word. It makes you warm. But you shouldn't use it too often—not you, Mendel. I like you, I like being with you, but don't think I've forgotten! We coachmen have excellent memories. If I see a face once, it stays with me forever. Well I've seen you before . . . I saw you the day you came to propose to us that we form this company—you belonged to no community then, did you? And when we asked you questions, you were silent. You wished to be alone—and you were. Even with us, you were alone. You never shared your past with us, you never opened up. What do we know about you? That you are a beggar. What were you before you became a beggar? What made you become a beggar? It's impossible to get a word out of you. You and your silences, you and your condescending attitudes, you and your isolation—you have never fooled me. And now you dare to talk about community?

MENDEL

Yes, I do. (*Sighs*) Before, I dared to stay on the sideline. Now I dare to move away from the sideline. And join. And you know what? For the same reasons.

YANKEL

What reasons?

MENDEL

I am not allowed to disclose them to you.

YANKEL

Why not? I want to know. As judge, I have the right to know.

MENDEL
(*To* AVRÉMEL)

You too?

AVRÉMEL

I know. But . . . I don't understand.

MENDEL

That's because of your profession. All your life you tried to entertain. To make people laugh. To do so, you had to learn to know them—not to understand them.

AVRÉMEL

And you?

MENDEL

I—I understood. I sought knowledge and acquired it. To safeguard that knowledge I withdrew from people. And ultimately it was that knowledge that shielded me. But it did not shield others. (*Pause*) What was the difference between the two of us? I didn't try to make people laugh.

MARIA

Try now! Please do!
(MARIA *is ignored by the three judges. She doesn't mind. She keeps busy cleaning glasses, wiping them, putting them away*)

AVRÉMEL

I did. I loved doing that. I loved seeing long, sad faces open up and become warm, good, human. I mean: beautiful; I mean: simple. I used to go from village to village, from one community to another, from one street to another, from synagogue to synagogue, yelling, "Anybody planning a wedding? Anybody contemplating an engagement? . . . No? Really not? . . . Why not? Can I change anyone's mind? . . . Yes? You said yes? Good! Bravo! *Mazel tov!* I am staying. I'll offer a special rate!" Ah, those were the good times . . . Do you know that occasionally people got married simply because I happened to be there? Even after, even during the pogrom, I ran through the streets and market places, through the cemeteries, calling, "Hey, good people, is there no wedding being planned? How about a marriage celebration while I am here?" I made the living cry. As for the dead, I may have made them laugh.

MENDEL
(*Dreaming*)

And God in all this?
64

AVRÉMEL

I don't know. Was He laughing or crying?

BERISH

Speaking of God, how about getting down to business?
(*His reminder brings them back to the present*)

MENDEL

You are right, innkeeper. (*To the others*) Ready?
(YANKEL *and* AVRÉMEL *nod*)

BERISH

One second, please. I have something to say.

MENDEL

We are listening, innkeeper.

BERISH

It's about my part. I want to choose it.

MENDEL

Why? Why you particularly?

BERISH

You mentioned freedom. To be free means to be able to choose.

MENDEL

It's all right with me. Go ahead, choose.

BERISH

Prosecutor. That's what I am going to be. Prosecutor.

MARIA

What's that?

AVREMEL

That's someone nice who has the right to be nasty.

BERISH

Tonight I want to be nasty.

MARIA

With whom?

BERISH

With everybody. And more.

MARIA

What will you get from it, Master?

BERISH

Satisfaction. That'll be enough. At last I want to be able to shout, yell, blame, insult, denounce, frighten whomever I please.

MENDEL
(*Consulting his two colleagues*)

I see no objection to that. Congratulations, innkeeper. The court has just appointed you prosecutor. Do you solemnly swear to faithfully and honestly fulfill your duties or . . . don't you?

BERISH

I do, except . . . except for "solemnly."

MENDEL

Ah?

BERISH
(*With a shrug*)

I don't like it.

MARIA

What's that?

BERISH

I don't know, but I don't like it.

66

MENDEL

How about "faithfully"?

BERISH

Yes.

MENDEL

How about "honestly"?

BERISH

Yes again.

MARIA

No!

MENDEL

No, Maria? Why do you say no?

MARIA

That's a word I *do* understand. And I know it's impossible.

MENDEL

Are you suggesting to this court that your master is dishonest?

MARIA

Did I say that? Did I say that my master is not honest? He is! But because he is honest, he cannot say "honestly"! Don't you see?

MENDEL

No, I do not.

MARIA

Really! How can he swear to do something honestly, when he's performing!

MENDEL
(*Smiles*)
All the court expects from him is to perform honestly.

YANKEL
A great day for you, innkeeper!

AVRÉMEL
Mazel tov, mazel tov! Congratulations! With the court's permission, I would like to compose a sonnet in his honor!

YANKEL
Let's celebrate!

MARIA
Again? They'll ruin us!

YANKEL
The occasion calls for drinks!

AVRÉMEL
Yes—the court so orders!

MARIA
The court, what's that?

MENDEL
You don't say "what," you say "who."

MARIA
Have it your way. Who is the court?

MENDEL
We are.

YANKEL
(*To* AVRÉMEL)
Mazel tov.
68

AVRÉMEL
(*To* YANKEL)
I know a song for all occasions:

> *Mazel tov, mazel tov,*
> Luck is with you
> *Mazel tov*
> And so is God
> *Mazel tov.*
> So taste the wine
> And forget the price,
> *Mazel tov . . .*

(MENDEL *silently reprimands him.* AVRÉMEL *bows respectfully*)

MENDEL
With your kind permission, Prosecutor, the court wishes to
introduce itself to you. We hope to fulfill our task with courage and wisdom. (*The two judges bow*) And you, Maria, what
part appeals to you?

MARIA
None. Unless you need a waitress . . . Oh, how silly of me.
I cannot play the waitress, since I am a waitress. Well, I want
no part at all.

MENDEL
Everybody plays some part . . .

MARIA
Then I'll play the audience.

AVRÉMEL
Congratulations, Maria! May your star rise and—

YANKEL
Mazel tov! It's simpler. You didn't know you'd get *such* an
important part, did you? Ah, if your mother could only be
here . . .

MARIA

My mother? Why drag her into this?

YANKEL

She would be so proud of you!

MARIA

He is completely crazy!

AVRÉMEL

Never mind, Maria, never mind. It's just an expression we used at home. When a good thing happened, we'd say, "Ah, if my mother could see me now."

MARIA

But she is half blind!

BERISH
(*Impatient*)

Let's forget her mother and remember what we are here for? Let's start!

MENDEL

But someone is missing.

BERISH

Who is that? The defendant? He's used to it.

MENDEL

I didn't mean Him; I meant His attorney.

MARIA

What's that? (*Corrects herself*) Who's that?

MENDEL

That's someone mean who has something nice to say about everybody.

BERISH

A flatterer.

MARIA

You mean someone who has the right to lie and flatter other liars?

MENDEL

Well said, Maria. Wouldn't you like to play that part?

MARIA

Oh no! I never lie and I never flatter! I'm being lied to— I'm being flattered: I'm the audience! I'm the masses!

MENDEL

But we *need* an attorney.

BERISH

I don't see why. Since we can do without the defendant, we could do without his attorney.

YANKEL

He is right.

AVRÉMEL

Oh no, sir. We must follow the rules. You may judge someone in his absence but not in the absence of his attorney. We must have a defense attorney in this court.

YANKEL

Obviously.

MENDEL
(*To* BERISH)

Sir?

BERISH

What do you want from me?

MENDEL

You represent authority. The power of the law. It is your duty to find a defense attorney for the defendant.

BERISH

I refuse.

MENDEL

You cannot do that, sir. It's against the rules.

BERISH

Sue me.

MENDEL

Watch your language, sir!

BERISH

Prosecutors watch other people's language! I say whatever I please, how I please. I am free and my freedom is unlimited!

MENDEL

Not so. Only the defendant's is. We are free only to accept or reject the rules of the game—to accept or refuse to play the game.

BERISH

Is that so? Then I won't play. Ladies and gentlemen, the show is over.

MENDEL

Are you threatening the court?

BERISH

Yes, I am. And that's only the beginning! You want to know what I intend to do next? I'll throw you out . . . (*He is ready to add new threats, has second thoughts*) Where do you expect me to get hold of a defense attorney? First, I don't know any. Second, there is none in Shamgorod. Third, even if there were, he wouldn't be Jewish. Lastly, I've nothing else to say.

(The prosecutor and the judges gaze at one another. Where are they going to go from here?)

AVRÉMEL

I want to say something.

YANKEL

Is it urgent?

AVRÉMEL

Always.

MENDEL

Only if it is related to the present debate.

AVREMEL

It is. The prosecutor urgently needs to be taught some manners.

BERISH

I protest! (MENDEL *looks quizzically at* AVRÉMEL) It's unheard of!

AVRÉMEL

May I continue?

MENDEL

Please. But, dear colleague, remember that as judges we are committed not to offend anyone.

AVREMEL

As judges, it's our duty to protect the dignity of this court. Therefore I'm asking the prosecutor not to scratch his beard when appearing before us: this is not a tavern, if I may say the obvious. Also, when addressing the court, Prosecutor, you're bound to show us consideration and respect, even though you are longing inwardly to break our bones. Yell until tomorrow, but not at us. Also, and in the same order of ideas, I—and we

73

—would appreciate it if you would begin or end, or both, every sentence with the customary expression: Your Honor!

BERISH
(*Doesn't understand*)

Your—what?

AVRÉMEL

Your Honor.

MARIA

What's that? Or is it, who's that?

BERISH

Tell me, are you *completely* insane or only mostly?

AVRÉMEL

He's insulted the court! I demand he be indicted for contempt!

BERISH

Maybe we need a doctor, not an attorney!

MARIA

We had a doctor. He was killed.

MENDEL

Prosecutor, please try to understand that my colleague's statement is not aimed at you personally.

BERISH

No? Then why did he talk to me?

MENDEL

He talked to you but he didn't mean to offend you.

BERISH

Whom then?

74

MENDEL

No one. All he meant to say is that there are certain customs and forms we must all adhere to.

BERISH

Not I! I don't know these customs and do not wish to know them!

MENDEL

What are you afraid of, Prosecutor? Listen, at home they called you Berish, right? (BERISH *nods*) Your customers call you innkeeper, right? In the synagogue they call you Reb Dov-Baer ben . . .

BERISH

Yaakov.

MENDEL

Yaakov. See? We address one another differently according to the place and to the circumstances that brought us together. So here, in the courtroom, you address us as Your Honor, that's all.

BERISH

And how will you address me?

MENDEL

Very respectfully, sir.

BERISH
(*Surmounts his hesitation*)
All right, if you say so . . . Your Honor.

MENDEL

Good! Excellent! You see? You learn fast! I compliment you on your amazing progress! Except we still don't have an attorney.

BERISH

To hell with him . . . Your Honor.
(YANKEL *and* AVRÉMEL *seem offended, but not* MENDEL)

MENDEL

We need an attorney; we cannot start our proceedings without one. You do understand that, don't you, sir?

BERISH

But there is no one to serve as attorney, don't *you* understand that? (*Stops to reflect*) Your Honor, must the attorney be a man?

MENDEL

Not necessarily.

BERISH
(*Moves toward* MARIA)

Maria!

MARIA

Oh no, Master. I'm the audience, remember? The people. And the people are more important than anyone. More important than attorneys. More important than prosecutors. And judges. You can do without Your Honor, but not without the people.

BERISH

What nonsense! You are not the people, you are you.

MARIA

Sorry, Master. Don't count on me.

BERISH

Do it for me.

MARIA

Sorry, Master. Don't get angry at the people; the people won't like it. The people want you to be gentle and tender—

BERISH

I'll kill you, you witch!

MARIA

Why? The people can say anything they please—

MENDEL

Right. Under one condition: that they do not say it.

BERISH

I'll kill her if she doesn't help me out, I'll kill her.

MARIA

Don't get angry, Master. I am not an attorney—I don't even know what an attorney looks like. I don't even know what he does, what he says. Must he believe in law and justice to defend them—or the opposite? You see, Master, I'm too ignorant. . . . And also, I'm not even Jewish!

YANKEL

Hmmm.

MENDEL

Is my illustrious colleague asking for the floor?

YANKEL
(*Clears his throat*)

My Honor wishes to tell Your Honor something very important.

MENDEL

The court will listen to you eagerly and sympathetically.

YANKEL

When Srulik the butcher needed my coach to bring him to Nadvorno, I told him that my horse was sick. So he brought his own.

So?

YANKEL

So I wonder whether we—the tribunal—couldn't ask the defendant to bring His own attorney. Or to be His own attorney.
(*Laughter*)

BERISH
(*Sneers*)

Ask Him, why not? What are you waiting for? (*He becomes serious*) Never mind. There are two possibilities: either we play without attorney or—we don't play at all!

ALL

Not at all! What a shame . . .

BERISH

Well, if you insist on the attorney, there is nothing we can do—except abandon the whole idea. I'll go to bed and you—out!
(*The threat is real, and all sense it. Their only chance to stay is to stage the play*)

ALL

No, no! Impossible!

MENDEL

Do you have a friend in the neighborhood?

BERISH

No. I told you, there are no more Jews around.

MENDEL

You, Maria? Can you think of anyone who might do?

78

MARIA
(*Hesitates*)

No . . . No.

BERISH
(*Nastily*)

Oh, she had somebody. But he left. (*Moves closer to* MARIA)
Look, she's blushing!

MARIA

Leave me alone, Master.

BERISH

Why are you blushing? He was a nice man. Strong and
handsome. Look! She's blushing! (*Pause*) He seduced you,
didn't he?

MARIA
(*Troubled, angry*)

Please, Master. Why do you want to hurt me?

BERISH

You spent the whole night with him, didn't you? You think
I didn't see you? I saw you in his arms . . . He left you. Why
did he leave you?

MARIA

This is not the time, Master . . . Please!

BERISH

What was his name?

MARIA

His name? . . . His name was—Sam.

BERISH

Sam—what?

MARIA

Just Sam.

BERISH

No last name?

MARIA

Only Sam.

BERISH

Lack of manners! He didn't introduce himself to you? And you let him take you? A stranger? (*To the court*) He appeared shortly before the pogrom, spent the night here and left in the morning. (*Pause*) He was a Jew, he spoke Yiddish to me. To her he spoke . . . What did he speak to you, Maria? You didn't speak, is that it?

MARIA

Master, I beg of you. Stop it.

BERISH

What did he promise you? What did he offer you? He would've been perfect for the job . . . for any job, I might say.

MARIA
(*Close to tears*)

Please, please! Stop talking about him!

BERISH

How *did* he seduce you? What did he tell you? What did he promise you?

MARIA

You're cruel, Master! God will punish you . . . He already has!

MENDEL

Have you seen him since? No? Do you know his where-
abouts?

MARIA

I beg you, old man, stop torturing me!

BERISH

But what about the damn attorney?! Because of him we'll
be deprived of a trial! (*To* MENDEL) Is there no way of getting
around the difficulty? How about . . . bribery? I've heard of
judges being bought, you know . . .

MENDEL

Wait. (*All stare at him*) Actually, in the ancient Jewish tradition, trials were conducted without defense attorneys—

BERISH
(*Exuberant*)

Good heavens, why didn't you remember that sooner?

MENDEL

—and without prosecutors.

BERISH
(*Shocked*)

You want to get rid of me already? Are you asking for my
resignation? If you oust me, I'll oust you. Just try it! With or
without Your Honor, you'll be in the street one-two-three!

MENDEL

Don't get excited, innkeeper! You're the best prosecutor
we've got. You see, in ancient times, when innkeepers were
innkeepers, judges were required to be able to handle both
the prosecution and the defense of an accused. But now, everything has changed, the legal system itself has changed. We
may therefore adapt it to our situation. Since we already have
a prosecutor, we will ask a member of this court to serve as
both judge and attorney for the defense.

81

BERISH

You are a genius! And so I offer you ten free meals begin-ning tomorrow—

YANKEL

Bribery, this is bribery!

BERISH

—and ten for you too.

YANKEL

Yes, as I was saying, this might appear to be bribery. But it isn't! For if it were, who would prosecute the prosecutor?

AVRÉMEL

Let's vote.

MENDEL

A suggestion has been made to appoint a member of this tribunal attorney for the accused, whose absence ought not be misinterpreted. Who is in favor?

YANKEL

Couldn't we vote *after* the meal? (*He looks at* MENDEL *ques-tioningly*) All right, I'm for it! And what about you, jester?

AVRÉMEL

I am hungrier than you.

MARIA

Ten meals . . . multiplied by three . . .

MENDEL

The audience is requested to keep its comments to itself.

MARIA

You mean you all may speak but I may not?

YANKEL

This woman keeps on interrupting our proceedings; I demand she be jailed and punished.

BERISH
(*To* MARIA)

Offer them twenty free meals, hurry!

MARIA

Twenty? Why twenty? You want them to stay a whole year?

MENDEL

Woman, you are under arrest.

MARIA

All right, twenty.

MENDEL

You're under arrest.

MARIA

I said twenty. That's not enough? All right—thirty.

MENDEL

Never mind. Just apologize to the court.

MARIA

I have the honor to tell Your Honor—and Yours—and Yours—that I am sorry for having doubted your honor.

MENDEL

We may proceed. (*To* AVRÉMEL *and* YANKEL) Who volunteers to serve as lawyer for the accused?

YANKEL

I know one thing—and I know it well; I know who will not volunteer: I.

MENDEL

You refuse?

YANKEL

I didn't say that. All I said is that I *know* who will not volunteer.

MENDEL

That means you refuse.

YANKEL

I speak of what I know; you speak of what you do.

MENDEL

But why, Yankel? To defend the Creator of all things, the Judge of all mankind, the King of Kings—is there a greater honor than that?

YANKEL

Thank you for bringing me customers. As a passenger, I would take Him: He doesn't take much room. Here it's different. First, I don't know what and if He'll pay. You'll tell me: could you be sure that He'd pay for his coach fare? No, I couldn't. But it's not the same thing. He'd sit in the coach and the horses would do the pulling; in court, I'd be the horse. So why do it at all? Second, and that's worse: Suppose I lose the case? No, it's not for me. Let someone else take this case.

MENDEL

And you, Avrémel?

AVRÉMEL

Yes, of course—I mean: no, of course not.

MENDEL

But in a way, it's your profession, isn't it? You were a minstrel. You know your way around with words. Make up a few for Him—why not?

84

AVRÉMEL

Such a client deserves a better attorney. I would only shame
Him. With me as lawyer, He risks finding himself in hell
. . . Oh, what am I saying? I hope He didn't hear me. If He
did, I will be the one who needs to be defended.

BERISH
(*Amused*)
There is one more candidate left. (*Pause*) You.

MENDEL

As president of this court, I declare that the president has
not been and *is* not a candidate.

BERISH

Why not?

MENDEL

As president, I don't have to tell you.

BERISH

I have the right to know.

MENDEL

And I have the right to deny you your right.

YANKEL

The prosecutor wants an explanation. So do we! We ex-
plained. Why don't you?

MENDEL

Because.

AVRÉMEL

That's not an answer?

MENDEL

Nothing is.

BERISH

I protest!

MENDEL

Good for you.

YANKEL

We all protest.

MENDEL

Good for you, too.

BERISH

Listen, beggar of my heart, you deny me the right to know, and this is unfair. What is the purpose of this trial? We know perfectly well that the outcome won't change anything: the dead will not rise from their graves. We judge because we wish to know. To understand. In order to understand others, I must understand you too! Speak up, for heaven's sake!

MENDEL

As president, I choose when to speak and when to keep quiet. Now I have chosen not to speak.

BERISH

I object!

MENDEL

Objection overruled.

MARIA

The people protest!

MENDEL

I shall have the courtroom evacuated if you persist!

MARIA

I protest—the people protest against your not letting me protest!

BERISH

Objection!

MARIA

More objections!

YANKEL

Booo!
> (*They shout and shout. Then, spent, they become motionless, silent*)

MENDEL

You forget why we have gathered here tonight? (*Pause*) The question remains a question: Is there no one here—or anywhere—to plead the cause of the Almighty King of the universe?
> (MENDEL *has spoken with nostalgia. Melancholy sets in*)

AVRÉMEL

Poor, poor King of Kings.

YANKEL

Feel sorry for Him? Already?

BERISH

We're heading in the wrong direction! We're here not to pity Him but to judge Him!

AVRÉMEL

Poor King who needs His servants' pity.

BERISH

He needs it? He won't get it! Not from me! He had no pity for me, why should I have for Him?

MENDEL

I—who? Berish the innkeeper or Berish the prosecutor?

BERISH

Berish is Berish.

MENDEL

But who is Berish? An innkeeper who plays the part of prosecutor, or a prosecutor who happens to be innkeeper?

BERISH

Don't confuse me. I am I. Isn't that enough for you?

MENDEL

Anyone can say "I."

BERISH

You confuse me. I protest.

YANKEL

I—who?

BERISH

I—Berish. And I'm fed up with you! I'm an honest man, I've never stolen, I've never cheated! I've never humiliated anyone! I have done only good, not He. He has done me nothing but harm. And now, now you want me to feel sorry for Him? Where was He when . . . (*Catches himself and tries to sound calm*) I forgot that we are playing—maybe He, too, is playing. (*To* MENDEL) Who are you when you're not playing? Tell me. I want to know.

MENDEL

Why?

BERISH

Say that I love to know the truth. About me—and you. And Him. And everyone else. I know what we're about to play but not with whom I'm about to play. Tell me.

YANKEL

Don't waste your energy on him; you'll get nowhere. He is a rich beggar; he has a secret treasure; his treasure is his secret.

BERISH

And you are not even curious to find out?

YANKEL

Questions are like trips: we must know when to stop. Coachmen have to think of their passengers. And the horses.

BERISH

Let them drop dead.

YANKEL

Who? The passengers?

BERISH

The horses.

YANKEL

What have they done to you?

BERISH

Nothing, nothing. *You* are annoying me, not they. You're all getting on my nerves! A nice Purim you've arranged for me!

MENDEL

You are asking too many questions, innkeeper. Purim is not the time for that. Purim is the story of Esther, and Esther means secrecy. Everything remains hidden, and it's not up to you to reveal it. You, as prosecutor, must bend before the law.

BERISH

I'm ready to bend before the law, but I insist on understanding it! I want to know what is happening and why!

89

MENDEL

So do we, innkeeper.

BERISH

But you are not I. I want to know why human beings turn
into beasts. So do you. But you haven't seen them. I want to
know how good family men can slaughter children and crush
old people.

MENDEL

So do we, innkeeper.
(BERISH *yields. His mood changes*)

BERISH

What strange birds you are. I don't know who you are, but
I know that you are strange. Where do you come from? Who
sent you? Who are you?

YANKEL

His curiosity will do him in, I am sure of that.

AVREMEL

He *is* going too far.

YANKEL

He is drunk, after all.

BERISH

Drunk? Me? Too easy. Why do you say that I am drunk?
Because I want to know who you are? Strangers make me feel
uneasy. They come and go, and I stay behind like an imbecile.
You'll tell me, what about the defendant? Isn't He a stranger
too? Yes, He is, but not really. I know Him, oh yes, I know
Him. In my own way, I know Him, all right. He is like a
customer; you don't need to know customers: you sell them
food and drinks; they go and I keep their money. But you are
not customers. You can't even pay your bill—you are something else and I want to know what.

Who.

BERISH

You're right, witch. Who, what, it's all the same. They're making fun of us.
> (MENDEL *examines him closely and begins to speak to him in the manner of a teacher talking to pupils. Gradually his voice rises and gains tension and anger*)

MENDEL

You are funny, Berish. The innkeeper yearns for justice, and the prosecutor will settle for knowledge. Have you forgotten what tradition has taught us? We must drink *Ad d'lo yada*—we are bound by law to drink and drink, and drink more, until we are unable to distinguish between good and evil, between Mordechai the Just and the wicked Haman, between light and shadow, life and death. Purim signifies absence of knowledge, refusal of knowledge. Are you going to change tradition? Establish a new one? On whose authority? (BERISH *makes a movement,* MENDEL *notices it*) Are you going to threaten once again to send us out into the street? Stop threatening! It won't work! You are no longer free to withdraw! Once the trial has begun, it has to be brought to a conclusion!

BERISH
(*Retreats*)

You are touchy, aren't you? All I wanted—

MENDEL

All you wanted was—what? What did you want? To begin at the end? To force us to prejudge the case? Enough of your diversionary tactics! We are dealing here with a unique case with unprecedented implications! Our judgment may prove useless but not meaningless! You want to know who we are? We are members of a rare tribunal whose authority derives from its own sense of justice and perhaps humor. You want to know more, and go to the end of all worlds; you want to tear off all that covers certain words, break the vessels of—

(*His violent tirade is interrupted by the* PRIEST*'s re-entrance. Sudden silence. Renewed fear*)

PRIEST

Maria, Maria, here I am again, you see? I need you. I need to save your soul—even if you reject me. Come, daughter. Come, give me another drink. I need strength to take care of your salvation. (*At* BERISH*'s signal,* MARIA *hands him a drink*) Yes . . . (*He addresses* BERISH *and the three Jews*) and of yours as well . . . You are in great danger, believe me. Heed my warning.

MARIA

You're repeating yourself, Father.

PRIEST

So does our Father in Heaven, Maria. So does He. How many times has He been repeating to us the teaching of His love? But you refuse to love Him, as you refuse to love me. Is it that you are unable to love altogether, Maria? It's because of your sinful adventure with the Stranger; I swear that it's that night that you lost your soul . . . Remember that night, Maria? I do. You were together, I saw you . . .

MARIA

You dirty pig—you Peeping Tom—and that claims to be God's servant!

PRIEST

You sinned, Maria. Remember, Maria, you let yourself be seduced by the Stranger, and punishment struck soon after, remember?

MARIA

It didn't strike me! It struck those who had not sinned! You better look for a better example!

PRIEST

I am not looking for any, not now, daughter. You think I
came back to preach? I came to help you. I want to help you.
Don't ask me why. Perhaps it's because I can't forget the last
time . . . It happened here, Maria. I was present. And you, too.
And Berish. And Hanna. And—

MARIA

Enough, Father!

PRIEST

I don't want it to happen again. I'm responsible for my flock
. . . I want to prevent further bloodshed. And there will be
bloodshed, believe me. There is hate. Hate leads to bloodshed. I came to you in the name of heavenly love.

YANKEL
(*To* AVRÉMEL)

How about inviting him to play in the show?

BERISH
(*To the* PRIEST)

We're grateful. Touched by your kindness. But we're busy.
Come back another day, another evening.

PRIEST

Another day? Will there be another day?

PRIEST

Some people always think they have time. They're on the
edge of the abyss and don't want see; they're singed by the
flames and don't realize that they're already in hell.

MARIA

Hell? Is he talking about hell? Good. For a moment I was
afraid he was making sense.

PRIEST

I am talking about hell because . . . because I always do. It's

a matter of habit. And it's easier. But you're wrong in not
listening . . .

BERISH
Another time. Do come back another time. Hell will wait,
I promise you.

PRIEST
But it's late, innkeeper. Much later than you think.

BERISH
Right you are! Much later! So go home, go back to bed.

PRIEST
Don't worry over me; I risk nothing. You do. You risk a
lot. I told you, didn't I? Go away. Take your family, your
friends, and go into hiding. In the woods. Anywhere. If
you've nowhere to go, come to my house—the House of the
Lord. (*Pause, then more gently*) You'll be in relative safety. It's
safer than here . . . Oh, I've not come back to convert you.
Be damned if that's your desire. But I want to protect you
from the mob. You must believe me, Berish, you must.

BERISH
You *have* become charitable all of a sudden! What has come
over you?

PRIEST
The mob is mine, Berish. I'm in charge of their souls. I don't
want to see them commit murder again. I saw enough the last
time.

MENDEL
Is the danger that imminent?

BERISH
Could anything happen *tonight?*

PRIEST

It's possible. Everything is possible. I've got a good nose.
I can smell bloodshed. I feel the mob getting ready.

MARIA

You have a nose, yes? And what about the last time? Where
was your nose then? Why didn't you warn us the last time?
(*Her hate is tangible, visible*)

BERISH

Maria!

PRIEST

You're right, Maria. I should have; I didn't. But then, I
tried to save you, Berish, didn't I? I did my best, didn't I?

BERISH

Yes, you did. You offered us the protection of the cross.

PRIEST

That was your best chance, Berish! If you had accepted,
your sons and their mother might still be alive!

BERISH

Enough! Not another word!

PRIEST

You're angry and I know why. We were friends and I
couldn't protect your family. But I am still your friend, more
than ever. You must listen to me. You must believe me!

MENDEL

You really think it could happen tonight?!

PRIEST

Yes.

MENDEL

But you're not sure?

PRIEST

No.

MENDEL

Then we will think about it.

PRIEST

When?

MENDEL

After the play.

PRIEST

After what?

MENDEL

After the play.

PRIEST

What? A mob is getting ready—knives are being sharpened
—and you're acting?

MENDEL

Outside, Haman's mob is getting ready, while inside, the
Jews went on with their prayers; that was their idea of theater.

PRIEST

May I stay and watch?

MENDEL

No, you may not.

PRIEST

Why not? Are you going to say bad things about me or my
people?

MENDEL

No, neither about you nor about your people.

96

PRIEST

What is the play about?

MENDEL

We don't know yet. It's going to be an improvisation.

PRIEST

Looking for ideas? How about staging a conversion? No?
A pity. What a pity.

MENDEL

Thank you for the suggestion, but—

PRIEST

I understand, I understand. (*Walks to the exit, stops*) No, I
do not understand. You, Berish—were you ever known for
your piety? Were you seen more often with drunkards or with
rabbis? Then tell me: Why this sudden loyalty to your God—
why?

MENDEL

Our relations with God are our business—ours alone.

MARIA

Is *he* preaching *here?* To you, Master? Where does he think
he is? In church?

MENDEL

There is the people of Israel and there is the God of Israel:
Let no one interfere in their affairs!

PRIEST

So, you forbid me to help you, to save you, is that it? All
right, then. Go and hand yourselves over to the sword. You'll
get what you deserve. Amen. (*Pause*) God doesn't love you
anymore, admit it. He has turned His face away from you.
Why don't you see the truth as it is? He is fed up with you.
He is disgusted with you . . .

MARIA

Wicked drunkard!

BERISH

(*To the* PRIEST)

Look who's talking! If someone is disgusting, it's you!

PRIEST

God, the God of your fathers, has given up on you. That's why He handed you over to us—the servants of Christ, His Son. From now on, we shall be your masters, your rulers; we shall be your God. Why would we be invested with such powers if it were not for God, who entrusted us with a mission to you, His rebellious children? It is the will of God that we, Christians, shall be your God.

MENDEL

That you are God's whip, that is quite possible. But don't be so proud of it! God is closer to the Just struck by the whip than to the whip. God may punish the Just whom He loves, but despise the instrument of punishment; He throws it in the garbage, whereas the Just will find his way to the sanctuary.

PRIEST

Don't go too far! You have just thrown into the garbage my Lord! He is the Son of God!

MENDEL

We all are.

PRIEST

You were once. He disowned you.

MENDEL

Are you certain of that? How can you be so sure? Because we suffer? Between the man who suffers and the one who makes him suffer, whom do you think God prefers? Between those who kill in His name and those who die for Him, who, in your judgment, is closer to Him?

PRIEST

Now you speak of Christ as an assassin! How dare you!

MENDEL

Wrong—you haven't been listening. I speak not of Christ but of those who betray Him. They invoke His teaching to justify their murderous deeds. His true disciples would behave differently; there are no more around. There are no more Christians in this Christian land.

PRIEST
(*Calm again*)

Is it His fault? Why blame Him? If what you say is true, then feel sorry for Him. If Christ is alone and abandoned—then it's up to you, His brethren, to comfort Him.

MENDEL

We will, Priest. One day we will.

PRIEST

One day, one day—you Jews love to see far ahead. Another day, another day. Not now, later. Then it's too late . . . Will you remember that I warned you?

(*He exits slowly. All the actors follow him with their eyes. He opens the door. The wind outside makes the candles flicker*)

MENDEL

What happened the last time, innkeeper?

BERISH

Forget it. I'm not going to tell you.

MENDEL

We would like to know.

BERISH

Too bad. Did you answer my questions? Why should I answer yours?

MENDEL

Maria . . .

BERISH

She won't answer you either!

MENDEL

Maria, perhaps you ought to go to the window from time to time. Keep watching. One never knows.

MARIA

The priest talks a lot, that's all.
> (*She would like to reassure her friends. They now feel the danger.* BERISH *also knows that there is no way to avoid it*)

BERISH

Can we return to the play?

MENDEL

No.

BERISH

Why not?

MENDEL

No defense attorney.

YANKEL

Don't count on me.

AVRÉMEL

Or me.

MARIA

You are all funny. When you want to accuse, you are here, ready to judge and pass sentence. But when you are asked to defend, you turn around and start running.

MENDEL

What about Hanna?

BERISH

What do you have in mind?

MENDEL

She could play the defense attorney.

BERISH

She's sick. Let her be. You don't ask a sick person to play
a sick person.

MARIA

Poor, poor Hanna. Does she realize what's happened?
What will happen?

BERISH
(*To the three judges*)

How about flipping a coin? Let fate decide.

YANKEL

I don't like it, but—

AVRÉMEL

I don't like it without but.

MENDEL

I could appoint one of you.

YANKEL

You can force a horse to run but not to neigh.

AVRÉMEL

You can force the coachman.

YANKEL

You cannot. But you can force a jester to sing.

AVRÉMEL

No. You cannot.

MENDEL

Then it's a deadlock.

MARIA

Who's that?

MENDEL

We are at a point from which it is impossible to proceed.
We are standing still.

MARIA

And waiting?

MENDEL

And giving up.

MARIA

The people says no.

YANKEL

Let the people keep quiet and say no later.

AVRÉMEL

Perhaps it's for the best. If the priest is right, then we could
use the time for more urgent things. For instance: we could
run.

YANKEL

And run fast!

MARIA

The people has changed its mind; I say yes. Let's start looking. Packing. Move out. The priest is drunk, but I don't have
too much faith in his drunkenness.

AVRÉMEL

So—we stop the play? And run?

YANKEL

We stop the play. Goodbye, Judge. Good evening, Minstrel. It'll be nice to meet you again.

MARIA

Let's go to the forest; we could at least lie down and rest. And gather some strength for tomorrow.
(YANKEL *and* AVRÉMEL *get up.* MENDEL *remains seated.* BERISH *sizes them all up and explodes*)

BERISH

All right, go! Go, all of you! Go to bed! Go to sleep! Have pleasant dreams! Cowards, imbeciles! Even to play against Him frightens you! Scared to open your mouths! The attorney? A convenient pretext. The rules? An excuse. In truth, you didn't dare continue! In truth, you were planning to stop in the middle from the very beginning! You were waiting for the right moment to run away with your heads lowered and your hearts full of contrition! I know your kind. Go away! Out of here, out of my sight! I don't need you! I'll play without you. I'll yell for truth all by myself! I'll howl words that have been howling inside me and through me! I'll tear off all the masks of Him whose face is hidden! With or without an attorney present, Your Honor, the trial will take place!

YANKEL

But, innkeeper, it's irregular!

AVRÉMEL

If there is a prosecutor, there must be a defense attorney!

BERISH

There is none—but who is to blame for that? His defenders? He killed them! He massacred His friends and allies! He could have spared Reb Shmuel the dayan, and Reb Yehuda Leib the cantor, and Reb Borukh the teacher, Hersh the sage, and Meilekh the shoemaker! He could have taken care of those who loved Him with all their hearts and believed in Him —in Him alone! Whose fault is it if the earth has become inhabited by assassins—by assassins alone?

MENDEL

By assassins alone? What about us? Our brethren? Are we assassins too?

BERISH

You are clowns, all of you. The earth is inhabited by assassins and clowns.

MENDEL

And Hanna? (*Pause*) And Hanna in all this?

BERISH

Yes, Hanna . . . Hanna, my daughter. I wanted to have the trial on her behalf. You have seen her. She is barely alive; you can't call that living. She sleeps, she sighs, she eats, she listens, she smiles; she is silent: something in her is silent. She speaks silently, she weeps silently; she remembers silently, she screams silently. At times when I look at her I am seized by a mad desire to destroy everything around me. Then I look at her again, closer, and a strange kindness comes over me; I feel like saving the whole world. I am ready to invite all people to come and eat, drink, sing and celebrate—and together drive away the curse that transforms certain people into killers and others into their victims . . . And listen to a clown who makes people laugh. And then, I realize that the clown, that's me.

(*He suddenly regrets having spoken. He shrugs and exits*)

MARIA

You didn't know him before. He was generous and warm toward everybody, Jews and Christians. His wife and I were like sisters. His two sons helped me build the hut for my old mother . . . Why did it have to happen, why?

MENDEL

What happened? *What* happened? Tell us!

MARIA

He has sealed my lips; why open them? Why open old
wounds? Can't you imagine what happened? This was a good
family, the best. Happiness was deserved and shared. Happiness, happiness . . . (MENDEL *looks at her, pleading with her*)
What do you want me to say? We were getting ready to
celebrate Hanna's wedding. The best cooks had prepared the
best meals. Wine, cake, fruit. Musicians, singers, comedians.
Seven holy rabbis had come' from faraway villages to partici-
pate in the ceremony. Hanna's beauty—how can I describe to
you Hanna's divine beauty? Whoever saw her had tears in his
eyes—tears of joy and gratitude. Whoever saw her couldn't
help but become her friend and protector. There were a hundred guests and more at the inn. Everyone was happy, everyone thanked God for being alive to witness his own happiness.
Then . . . *they* arrived. They broke everything. Pillaged all the
rooms. Killed the two boys, Hayim and Sholem. Slaughtered
all the guests. Beheaded the mistress of the house. And Hanna
—they began torturing Hanna. They did things to the poor
child. It lasted for hours and hours.

(*She stops*)

MENDEL

Please, Maria, go on.

MARIA

That's all you need to know. That's all there *is* to know.

MENDEL

And the innkeeper?

MARIA

I don't understand.

MENDEL

You told us what happened to Hanna, her brothers and their mother—but not what *they* did to their father.

MARIA

The master fought them with all his strength; he used a hatchet, kitchen knives and clubs; he wounded a few assailants, but he was outnumbered: one against twenty, thirty—more.

MENDEL

Then? What happened then?

MARIA

Nothing.

MENDEL

Go on, Maria! I'm ordering you to continue!

MARIA

I refuse to obey your orders! (*Becomes humble again*) They tied him to the table. Poured wine and alcohol into his throat. And forced him to look.

MENDEL

So he looked. What did he see?

MARIA

I don't know what he saw. Even if I knew, I wouldn't tell you. You have imagination? Use it. Imagine the worst.

MENDEL

I prefer knowing.

MARIA

It's your problem.
(*At this point the door opens. No one notices the* STRANGER. *He listens but does not move forward*)

MENDEL

We want to know, Maria. We must. Perhaps we have been sent here tonight for the sole purpose of learning what happened.

MARIA

You may try, but you'll never succeed. Nobody will. Look here, I was there—and I don't know.

MENDEL

Did you see the innkeeper?

MARIA

Yes, I saw him. I saw what he saw. I cried. I howled like a thousand howling dogs. Not that it mattered. The mob was amused. Excited. The louder I yelled, the more they enjoyed what they were doing.

MENDEL

And the innkeeper?

MARIA

He twisted and twisted; he looked and looked, and I shouted and yelled, and the beasts sneered, and little Hanna was covered with blood. Did she know who assaulted her first? And how many followed? It lasted an hour or two, and more, it lasted a whole lifetime, and they left.

MENDEL

You stayed.

MARIA

Of course I did. The priest did too.

MENDEL

The priest?

MARIA

Yes, he came in the middle of the assault.

MENDEL

Didn't he try to stop them?

MARIA

He did. They refused to listen. They were drunk. And busy raping. Pillaging. Murdering. While the beasts were shedding blood, while they ravaged Hanna's body and soul, he lifted his cross—the big one, the one he uses for special occasions—and spoke about love—heavenly love. Nobody listened. They would not have listened to Jesus in person.

MENDEL

And the innkeeper?

MARIA

He kept on staring, staring.

MENDEL

You too?

MARIA

Yes, I stared too. What else could I have done? The beasts kept on raping and exploding with pleasure, the priest kept on drinking and preaching, Hanna kept on suffering more and more pain and shame, the master was shedding tears of blood, and I kept on howling, howling—
(*She stops abruptly;* BERISH *has returned onstage*)

MENDEL
(*To* BERISH)
Now I no longer imagine; now I know.

BERISH

You think you know; you don't. You never will.

MENDEL

We stay with you, innkeeper. The trial will be held.

YANKEL

But . . . what about the attorney?

MENDEL

Oh yes, the defense attorney.

AVRÉMEL

Misery of miseries . . . In the whole wide world, from east to west, from south to north, is there no one to plead on behalf of the Almighty? No one to speak for Him?

YANKEL

No one to justify His ways?

AVRÉMEL

No one to sing His glory?

MENDEL

Poor King, poor mankind—one is as much to be pitied as the other . . . In the entire creation, from kingdom to kingdom and nation to nation, is there not one person to be found, one person to take the side of the Creator? Not one believer to explain His mysteries? Not one teacher to love Him in spite of everything, and love Him enough to defend Him against His accusers? Is there no one in the whole universe who would take the case of the Almighty God?

STRANGER

Yes. There is someone. (*Pause*) I will.
(*General commotion. The* STRANGER *smiles.* MARIA *stifles a scream, covering her mouth with both hands*)

109

MENDEL

Who are you? What do you want?

YANKEL and AVRÉMEL

Who sent you?

STRANGER

I am the one you have been looking for.
(BERISH *stays close to* MARIA, *as if to defend her*)

MENDEL

The court is in session!

CURTAIN

Act Three

Exactly the same as before. Still perturbed, the three judges cannot take their eyes off the STRANGER. *There is something about him that hurts them, almost physically. As for* MARIA, *she seems to withdraw into herself; she is afraid to look at the* STRANGER *or be seen by him.*

MENDEL

Who are you?

STRANGER

My name would mean nothing to you. Call me Sam.

MENDEL

Sam what?

STRANGER

Just Sam.

MENDEL

No family name?

SAM

No family.

MENDEL

No family? Impossible! Surely you have—or had—a father, a mother? Where are they? Where do you come from?

SAM

Must you ask? Must you know? You need a defense attorney and here I am.

BERISH

Have we met before?

SAM

Possibly. I have met many people in many places.

BERISH

Have you been a guest here?

SAM

Possibly. I have been a guest in many homes. You have customers, so do I. Some remember me, others prefer to forget me.

BERISH

I have a strange feeling of having seen you somewhere—here perhaps . . .

YANKEL

Me too. Perhaps in Drohobitz?

SAM

Perhaps.

AVRÉMEL

Perhaps in Amdour?

SAM

Perhaps.

YANKEL

In Kamenetz? Yes, in Kamenetz.

BERISH

Here—

SAM

It's possible. Everything is. I told you: I travel a lot. I meet

114

many people. That's my favorite pastime: to meet people. I like variety. I like to please. To gamble. To win.

MENDEL

What is your occupation?

SAM

Why do you insist on details? Whether I do other things as well, that is my business and, with all due respect, mine alone. If you want another attorney, tell me and I'll be on my way!

MENDEL

No, of course not. Except that we would like to know more about you.

SAM

You all have your little secrets—am I not entitled to mine?
(*The conversation has established a certain rapport between the newcomer and the others. They are willing to accept him. Most of the suspicion has subsided. In a moment they will ask him to play his part. Then, all of a sudden,* MARIA *lets out a scream*)

MARIA

Don't! Don't trust him! Not him! He's mean, evil! Don't let him close! He's Satan himself! I swear it on the life of the Lord! And on my own! He is Satan!
(*All are startled*)

BERISH

I knew it . . . I was right! I knew that my memory wouldn't fool me—

MARIA

Send him away! Good people, I beg you, throw him out before it's too late!

MENDEL

Berish, Maria . . . what are you talking about?

BERISH

I saw him only briefly—a fleeting glimpse—in the darkness, but I was right! Now everything is clear.

MENDEL

What is clear?

MARIA

He has no heart, no soul, no feeling! He's Satan, I'm telling you!

BERISH
(*To* MENDEL)

Don't you understand? They knew each other.

MENDEL

So what? She must have met many customers here.

BERISH

They knew each other intimately.

MENDEL
(*To* SAM)

Did you?

SAM

Indeed we did.

MENDEL

That changes everything. No, it changes nothing. So they knew each other—what's wrong with that? Is that a reason for us to disqualify him? He had an affair. With whom? With a member of the court? No. With the defendant perhaps? No. So what's the problem?

MARIA

You don't know. You don't know who he is—what he is,
what he is capable of doing. I know.

MENDEL

Tell us.

MARIA

He is evil. Cruel. He's not human. I'm telling you, he's not
human.

BERISH

It's him, I knew it. I had a glimpse of him just before
. . . before . . .
     (MARIA *is hysterical. The* STRANGER *is unmoved, slightly*
     amused)

MENDEL

What does this have to do with the trial?

BERISH

I believe Maria.

MENDEL

You are accusing him of what? What happened, Maria? Tell
us. We are your friends.

MARIA

Don't listen to him. Get rid of him. It's bad luck to have him
around.

SAM

Who is on trial here? You decide.

MARIA

Don't listen! Don't listen to him! It's dangerous even to
hear his voice! He perverts the soul and poisons the mind!

117

MENDEL

But why? Why, Maria?

SAM

Tell them, beautiful Maria. Tell them everything.

MARIA

No! I'm too ashamed!

SAM

You ought to be. But you were not then—were you? (*Pause*)
Can we act like civilized adults? Please tell this hysterical
peasant to keep quiet.

BERISH
(*Jumps at him*)
Now you insult her! You've hurt her, and now you insult
her! I remember now: she cried, she wept, she was not herself.
You destroyed her, and now—

SAM

Innkeeper, innkeeper, you protect her too much. Why do
you protect her so much?

BERISH

You dare to insinuate! One more word, and it'll be your
last!

MENDEL

Please, Berish. Please! He hasn't blamed you for anything
—why get excited over a joke? You were joking, right?

SAM

Always, Your Honor. I'm always joking.

MARIA
(*Contains her tears*)
Don't believe him, don't!

MENDEL

If you are not going to tell us everything, you will have to remain silent, Maria.

(MARIA *lets herself fall on the bench, her face in her hands. The* STRANGER *observes her with exaggerated pity*)

SAM

(*To break the mood*)

Let's have another drink, gentlemen. We all need it. Don't worry, innkeeper. I will pay. It's on me.

(SAM *pours drinks. The tension is broken*)

YANKEL

Ah, women! All the same! First they enjoy, then they cry.

AVRÉMEL

I knew some who cried all the time.

YANKEL

Perhaps they enjoyed crying.

AVRÉMEL

I saw them at weddings.

YANKEL

I saw them afterwards—

MENDEL

Enough of this! We are not at the circus!

YANKEL

A pity. A circus has horses.

AVRÉMEL

And bears that dance like people who dance like bears.

YANKEL

Really? I saw only horses; I see horses everywhere.

AVRÉMEL

Also tigers. And lions. And bearded women. And giant dwarfs.

SAM

And judges. And prosecutors. And defendants.

ALL

How dare you? Insolent man!

SAM

Isn't this a circus . . . of sorts?

MENDEL

No. It's theater. There is a difference.

SAM

Really? What is it?

MENDEL

A circus employs only clowns.

SAM

So does the theater.

MENDEL

At the circus you laugh even when you cry.

SAM

At the theater too.

MENDEL

A circus is for children; theater is not.

SAM

I would have preferred to appear at the circus . . . But tonight theater will do.

AVRÉMEL

Can you sing?

SAM

Occasionally I do. But only reluctantly.

AVRÉMEL

How sad.

MENDEL

Who are you?

BERISH

Haven't you heard? He's the stranger who—

MENDEL

—had an affair with—

BERISH

—who was here before—

MENDEL

Who are you when you are not a stranger? (*Pause*) To whom are you not a stranger?

YANKEL

I've seen him somewhere. It must have been in Drohobitz!

AVRÉMEL

Amdour.

MENDEL

All right, we will respect your right to privacy. But do you know what we intend to do here tonight?

SAM

I heard you say a few sentences before; I guessed the rest.

MENDEL

Do you know what we expect from you?

SAM

To fulfill my duties as defense attorney.

MENDEL

Do you know on behalf of whom?

SAM

Yes, I do.

MENDEL

And you are not intimidated?

SAM

I am never intimidated.

MENDEL

You are ready to defend your client, just like that, without the slightest hesitation—without any preparation whatsoever? Without asking yourself if perhaps you are not up to what is being demanded of you? (*Pause*) You are not even awed? (*Pause, then louder*) You feel nothing?

SAM

I dislike emotions. I prefer facts and cool logic. As far as I am concerned, we could open the proceedings right now. My client and I are ready.

MENDEL

How about you, Prosecutor?

BERISH

I am ready.

MENDEL
(*Bangs on the table*)

Under the authority vested in us, I open this grave and

solemn trial. We shall listen to the accusation and hear the defense. And we swear that justice will be done.

SAM

Justice? Whose justice? Yours?

BERISH

What kind of question is that? Justice is justice. Mine, yours, his: it's the same everywhere. Is there another?

SAM

There is that of God.

BERISH

And it isn't mine? If that is so, then, with your permission —or without it—I reject it, and for good! I don't want a minor, secondary justice, a poor man's justice! I want no part of a justice that escapes me, diminishes me and makes a mockery out of mine! Justice is here for men and women—I therefore want it to be human, or let Him keep it!

SAM

You want to reduce God's justice to yours? Why not elevate yours to His?

MARIA

Look at him! He's talking of justice! The scoundrel, the dirty scoundrel!

MENDEL

Maria! I forbid you!

BERISH

Let her speak! Why shouldn't the victims of injustice take part in a debate over justice?

SAM

The prosecutor had better learn the rules and procedures of the courtroom.

BERISH

Don't tell me what to learn and from whom!

YANKEL
(*Excited*)

Good, very good! Go on, quarrel!

AVRÉMEL

Louder!

YANKEL

Shout! Shout, I'm telling you!

AVRÉMEL

Let your words fight one another!

SAM

My client abhors violence, Your Honor. My client believes
in peace!

BERISH

Ha ha ha! He preaches peace and produces violence!

YANKEL

Good, Berish! Bravo, innkeeper!

AVRÉMEL

How about fighting in rhymes?

BERISH

Are you insane? Are we here to make rhymes?

YANKEL

We're here to celebrate Purim.

AVRÉMEL

And judge the wicked. And reward the just. In rhymes.

124

YANKEL

Purim . . . My horse used to neigh in rhymes, but only on Purim!

AVRÉMEL

Should we wear our masks?

YANKEL

You are a genius.

SAM

Your Honor!
(*Shows his displeasure*)

MENDEL

I would ask my distinguished colleagues to behave with more dignity! (*Also shows his displeasure*) And Prosecutor, to the point! Please!

SAM

We would deeply appreciate it if the prosecutor would spell out his accusations! What exactly are the charges?

MENDEL
(*To* BERISH)

Prosecutor?

BERISH

I—Berish, Jewish innkeeper at Shamgorod—accuse Him of hostility, cruelty and indifference. Either He dislikes His chosen people or He doesn't care about them—period! But then, why has He chosen us—why not someone else, for a change? Either He knows what's happening to us, or He doesn't wish to know! In both cases He is . . . He is . . . guilty! (*Pause. Loud and clear*) Yes, guilty!
(*Now the mood has changed. It contains violence.* BERISH *and* SAM *face each other in defiance.* SAM *displays irony;* BERISH, *anger. The court is solemn, uncomfortable*)

SAM

Guilty. No less. And you reached that conclusion all by yourself. Let's be serious. You, Prosecutor, are merely a person, whereas my client is—how shall I put it?—more than that. You wish to indict Him? So be it—but then, give us more than anger; give us evidence—that's what counts in a court of law, you know.

BERISH

Evidence? What's that?

SAM

Facts.

BERISH

Facts? What other facts do you want—what other facts do you need? We *are* the facts—we *are* proof, living proof. Look at us! (*Moves closer to him, threatening*) Look at us, and you'll know, and you'll understand. Look well—for we're the only ones you can still see in Shamgorod! The others, all the others are invisible. Absent. Dead. Look at us, I'm telling you, and you'll remember the others!

SAM

I am looking at you, and I see people very much alive, well fed, with no visible marks of poverty. You feed your guests, you offer them lodging—what are you complaining about?

MENDEL

The prosecutor does not complain; he accuses—

SAM

Whom? On what grounds? What does he want?

BERISH

Nothing. I had everything, and everything was taken away from me. But that's besides the point.

SAM

What *is* the point?

BERISH

Don't push me: I want the truth to be told.

SAM

Whose truth?

BERISH

Are we starting all over again? Whose truth? Mine! But if mine is not His as well, then He's worse than I thought. Then it would mean that He gave us the taste, the passion of truth without telling us that this truth is not true!

SAM

You wanted Him to tell you everything and do everything for you? He gave you passion—be thankful for that!

BERISH

Thankful! Shame on you and shame on Him for even suggesting that! He gave us suffering, that's what He gave us!

SAM

I know, I know. You have suffered and you are suffering still, and I sympathize, but pain does not constitute judicial evidence.

BERISH

All right. You've got one fact already. Shamgorod. Last year Shamgorod was a village with a Jewish community, a Jewish life. Shamgorod had a Jewish past and a Jewish future. Jewish warmth and Jewish songs could be found here in every street, in every house. Go look for them now. Shamgorod is mute. Its silence—what is it if not a fact? Three houses of study —demolished, pillaged; the main synagogue—burned down; the sacred scrolls—profaned. Aren't the ruins facts? Aren't the ashes glowing with facts? Over a hundred Jewish families lived here; now there is one—and this one is mutilated, maimed,

127

deprived of joy and hope. What is all this to you—and Him?
(*He raises his hand, as if ready to strike the adversary*) What is this,
I'm asking you?

SAM

Sad.

BERISH

What did you say?

SAM

Sad. It is sad.

MENDEL

Is that *all* you have to say?

SAM

Oh, I do not dispute the events, but I consider them to be
highly irrelevent to the case before us, Your Honor. I do not
deny that blood was shed and that life was extinguished, but
I am asking the question: Who is to blame for all that? After
all, the situation seems to me simple indeed: men and women
and children were massacred by other men. Why involve, why
implicate their Father in Heaven?

BERISH

You want to leave Him out? Turn Him into a neutral by-
stander? Would a father stand by quietly, silently, and watch
his children being slaughtered?

SAM

By whom? By his other children!

BERISH

All right, by his other children! Would he not interfere?
Should he not?

SAM

You are using images, let me add mine. When human beings kill one another, where is God to be found? You see Him among the killers. I find Him among the victims.

BERISH

He—a victim? A victim is powerless; is He powerless? He is almighty, isn't He? He could use His might to save the victims, but He doesn't! So—on whose side is He? Could the killer kill without His blessing—without His complicity?

SAM

Are you suggesting that the Almighty is on the side of the killer?

BERISH

He is not on the side of the victim.

SAM

How do you know? Who told you?

BERISH

The killers told me. They told the victims. They always do. They always say loud and clear that they kill in the name of God.

SAM

Did the victims tell you? (BERISH *hesitates*) No? Then how do you know? Since when do you take the killers' word for granted? Since when do you place your faith in them? They are efficient killers but poor witnesses.

BERISH

You would like to hear the victims? So would I. But they do not talk. They cannot come to the witness stand. They're dead. You hear me? The witnesses for the prosecution are the dead. All of them. I could call them, summon them a thousand times, and they would not appear here before you. They are not accustomed to taking a walk outside, and surely not on Purim eve. You want to know where they are? At the cemetery. At the bottom of mass graves. I implore the court to consider their absence as the weightiest of proofs, as the heaviest of accusations. They are witnesses, Your Honor, invisible and silent witnesses, but still witnesses! Let their testimony enter your conscience and your memory! Let their premature, unjust deaths turn into an outcry so forceful that it will make the universe tremble with fear and remorse!

SAM

Too easy, Your Honor. What gives the prosecutor the right to speak for the dead?

BERISH

I knew them alive. I witnessed their death.

SAM

So what? Does he know, is he empowered to know what they felt and thought and believed when they died? He depicts them as accusers—or witnesses for the prosecution. What if they felt differently? Suppose they chose, at that supreme hour, to repent! Suppose they were pleased—yes, pleased—to leave this ugly planet behind them and enter a world of eternal peace and truth?

BERISH

That's too much! Even for him! (*To* SAM) You really believe that people want to die, love to die? That they are happy to die? Either you're crazy or cynical! Woe to God if you're His defender!

SAM

I would like the court to remind the prosecution of its obligation not to indulge in personal attacks and insults! Does he wish to see me dismissed?

BERISH

But *he* is insulting the dead!

SAM

Why is that an insult? I would go one step further and say

130

that they departed from this world uttering words of gratitude—

BERISH

For what? For being slaughtered?

SAM

—for dying without prolonged suffering or shame. There are a thousand ways in which men die, you know.

BERISH

A lie, it's a lie! There are a thousand ways to suffer, but only one way to die—and death is always cruel, unjust, inhuman.

SAM

No, my dear Prosecutor. In these matters I am a greater expert than you. There are moments of death more cruel than others.

BERISH

You're telling me? More cruel, yes! Less cruel, no! (*To the court*) Take Reb Hayim the scribe, who never squashed a fly or an ant, for they too are God's living creatures; I saw him in agony. I want to know: Who willed his agony? Take Shmuel the cobbler, who treated strangers as though they were his own children; I saw his tears, his last tears. I demand an answer: Who was thirsty for his blood? I want to know: Why was Reb Yiddel the cantor murdered? or Reb Monish his brother? Why were Hava the orphan and her little brother Zisha murdered? So that they could say thank you—and I could say thank you?

SAM

Again you speak for them? You act as though they had appointed you their spokesman. Have they? You knew them —so what? Alive, they were yours; dead, they belong to someone else. The dead belong to the dead, and together they form an immense community reposing in God and loving Him the way you have never loved and never will! (*To the court*) He is asking, Why murder—why death? Pertinent questions. But we have some more: Why evil—why ugliness? If God chooses not to answer, He must have his reasons. God is God, and His will is independent from ours—as is His reasoning.

MENDEL

What is there left for us to do?

SAM

Endure. Accept. And say Amen.

BERISH

Never! If He wants my life, let Him take it. But He has taken other lives—Don't tell me they were happy to submit to His will—don't tell me they're happy now! If I'm not, and I'm alive, how can they be? True, they are silent. Good for them and good for Him. If they choose to be silent, that's their business! I shall not be!

SAM

That is understandable. They saw His charity and grace; you did not.

BERISH

Maria, you are right. He *is* repulsive. (*To* SAM) How can you speak of grace and charity after a pogrom?

SAM

Is there a more propitious time to speak about them? You are alive—isn't that a proof of His kindness?

BERISH

The Jews of Shamgorod perished—isn't that a proof of His lack of kindness?

SAM

You are obsessed with the dead; I only think of the living.

BERISH

And what if I told you that He spared me not out of kindness but out of cruelty?

SAM

He spared you, and you are against Him.

BERISH

He annihilated Shamgorod and you want me to be for Him? I can't! If He insists upon going on with His methods, let Him —but I won't say Amen. Let Him crush me, I won't say Kaddish. Let Him kill me, let Him kill us all, I shall shout and shout that it's His fault. I'll use my last energy to make my protest known. Whether I live or die, I submit to Him no longer.

SAM

He spared you, and you anger Him. He spared you, and you hurt Him, you make Him suffer.

BERISH

Don't talk to me of His suffering—leave that to the priest. If I am given the choice of feeling sorry for Him or for human beings, I choose the latter anytime. He is big enough, strong enough to take care of Himself; man is not.

SAM
(*With some warmth*)
What do you know of God that enables you to denounce Him? You turn your back on Him—then you describe Him! Why? Because you witnessed a pogrom? Think of our ancestors, who, throughout centuries, mourned over the massacre of their beloved ones and the ruin of their homes—and yet they repeated again and again that God's ways are just. Are we worthier than they were? Wiser? Purer? Are we more pious than the rabbis of York, the students of Magenza? More privileged than the dreamers of Saloniki, the Just of Prague and Drohobitz? Do we possess more rights than they did over heaven or truth? After the destruction of the Temple of Jerusa-

lem, our forefathers wept and proclaimed *umipnei khataenou*—it's all because of our sins. Their descendants said the same thing during the Crusades. And the Holy Wars. The same thing during the pogroms. And now you want to say something else? Does the massacre of Shamgorod weigh more than the burning of the Sanctuary? Is the ruin of your homes a more heinous crime than the ransacking of God's city? Does the death of your community imply a greater meaning than the disappearance of the communities of Zhitomir, Nemirov, Tlusk and Berditchev? Who are you to make comparisons or draw conclusions? Born in dust, you are nothing but dust.

BERISH

If He wanted me to be dust, why hasn't He left me as dust? But I'm not dust. I'm standing up, I'm walking, thinking, wondering, shouting: I'm human!

SAM

So were our ancestors.

BERISH

And they kept quiet? Too bad—then I'll speak for them, too. For them, too, I'll demand justice. For the widows of Jerusalem and the orphans of Betar. For the slaves of Rome and Capadoccia. And for the destitute of Oman and the victims of Koretz. I'll shout for them, against Him I'll shout. To you, judges, I'll shout, "Tell Him what He should not have done; tell Him to stop the bloodshed now. Discharge your duties without fear!"

MENDEL

We shall discharge our duties, innkeeper, but it will not be without fear.

SAM

Duties, duties . . . what big words . . . Your duties as what? As judges or as Jews?

134

MENDEL

Are the two incompatible?

SAM

The judges judge; Jews are being judged.

MENDEL

By whom?

SAM

First by God, then by other nations. We are in exile, you know.

BERISH

In exile, yet free! Members of the court, answer me: Are you free? I know it's all a game—it's theater; but within this game, are you free? Do you act the part of free men? Answer me!

> (*He is staring at the three judges with such anxiety that they are unable to reply; it takes them a minute to take hold of themselves*)

MENDEL

Tonight we are all free.

SAM
(*Laughs disquietingly*)

In some communities there is a custom of crowning a fool King of Purim. He is given a queen. Their kingdom lasts but one day, one night.

MENDEL

One night will be enough; it will be more than nothing—the opposite of nothing.

SAM

You are free—and what are you going to do with your freedom?

MENDEL

We shall be free—we shall judge freely—that will be all.

SAM

Will you judge without preconceived ideas?

MENDEL

Yes.

SAM

Without prejudice?

MENDEL

Yes.

SAM

Without passion?

MENDEL

No. With passion.

SAM

The verdict will be worthless!

MENDEL

It may be worthless, but it will be handed down neverthe-less.

MARIA
(*Rises*)

Even if you have a living witness? (*Pause*) If you have an eyewitness, will the verdict still be worthless?

MENDEL

Aren't you the audience? You have no right to intervene in the debate.

MARIA

I changed my mind. I want to testify.
(*She moves forward to face the court. As witness, she seems more determined, almost vengeful*)

MENDEL

Why, Maria? Why did you change your part—and your mind?

MARIA

You need a witness? Here I am. I have seen everything. I can testify, I have the right to. The duty as well.

SAM

I am not sure.

MENDEL

What do you mean? Why should her testimony not be accepted?

SAM

Well . . . she is not even Jewish.

BERISH

Are you? And even if you are, what difference does it make? Since when may witnesses be disqualified because of their religion? They must be honest—that's all. And I, Berish, the innkeeper of Shamgorod, vouch for her honesty.

MENDEL

Do you swear that you will tell the truth and nothing but the truth?

MARIA

Of course I do. But not the whole truth. The whole truth cannot be told—and yet I know the truth.

SAM

We have a Purim court—now we have a Purim witness!

MENDEL

You are intimidating the witness!

SAM

Listen, Your Honor, I was not going to tell you—I did not want to embarrass her in public, but since you insist . . . She is not what one might call an honorable woman. I would even go a step further and say that she is not what one might call a respectable woman.

BERISH
(*With hardly contained violence*)

You dirty swine!

SAM

No, not me; she is dirty. I wasn't going to say aloud what people say in whispers, but this is a court of law. The truth must be told.

BERISH

I'll strangle you with my own hands!

MARIA
(*To* BERISH)

Let him speak. (*She bites her lips*) Yes, Berish. I want to hear him speak.

BERISH

What for? I can do without his lies.

MARIA

So can I. Still, I want to hear them.

SAM

Lies? Must they be lies? Are you sure they will be? Members of the court, I owe you the truth: I have known this woman.

MENDEL

That much we guessed.

SAM

With the court's permission, I would like to explain the circumstances of our meeting—no, of our involvement. I came to spend the night here. I paid for space above the stove. I was alone. Not for long, though. I was half awake when I felt someone looking at me in the dark. Then she lay down next to me. Next to me? No, close to me. Closer. I could hardly understand what was happening when she began doing what honorable and respectable women must never do. She seduced me, members of the court. I resisted, I swear I did, but she knows how to get to men and weaken their resolve. She has had experience . . . And you were ready to receive her testimony!

BERISH

Dirty, dirty swine! I'll break your bones! Just wait!

SAM

I understand your anger—I would not have believed either that this woman could be so indecent and lack so much . . . restraint.

BERISH

(*Ready to attack him*)

Stop it!

SAM

Do you think I am inventing this?

BERISH

What do I think? That you're lying, that's what I think.

SAM

I am not, innkeeper. She and I—we spent a long night together. You do not believe me? Ask her. (*To* MARIA) Did we spend a long, delightful night together, yes or no?

(MARIA *is transfixed. It is as though she could not believe her own ears*)

MARIA
(*Still staring at* SAM)

Yes.

SAM

Near the stove?

MARIA

Yes.

SAM

Did you feel . . . pleasure?

MARIA

I did.

SAM
(*To* BERISH)

Well?

BERISH

You used force!

SAM
(*To* MARIA)

Did I?

MARIA

No.

BERISH

Don't tell me you charmed her! You used sorcery . . .

SAM

Ask her.

MARIA

He did. I knew much happiness with him—I would never
have guessed so much happiness existed.

140

(SAM shrugs off BERISH's outbursts. All eyes are on MARIA. Transformed. Tender as never before. Is she dreaming?)

MARIA

Evil—is there no limit to evil? It's like pain. So much pain then, and yet some was left for now. I don't understand why . . . Walks in the field. Whispers. Silences. Timid caresses. He spoke of his love for me. He couldn't live without me. It was the first time anyone spoke to me like that. "But I've just met you," I said. Yes, but he'd seen me. Many times. From far, far away. A relative's house, a friend's farm. But— no but. I ran, he ran after me. I refused to listen, I heard nevertheless. "That's love," he said. It was the first time I believed it is possible to be madly in love. Words, more words. More meetings at night. Words—I began waiting for them. My life was empty, empty of certain words. His made my blood run faster. Set my mind on fire. . . . Words became caresses. I was confused. Disturbed. Couldn't think or see. "Love," he kept on saying. "Love justifies everything." I was afraid of the word "everything"; also of the word "love." But— no but. One evening I ran away from him. To my room. And forgot to lock the door.

SAM
(Sneers)

How convenient . . .

MARIA

He opened it. Said he couldn't live without me. Cried and laughed. Threatened and promised. All the while whispering, whispering that love is more precious than life itself . . . His hands. His face. His lips. On me. In me. A scream. His? Mine? I thought, Love, that's what they call love. *(Long pause. No one, not even SAM, dares interrupt her recollection)* Then . . . the awakening. The change. He stood up and hit me in the face. With anger. And hate. "You cheap harlot," he shouted. "You fell for it, you really did!" More blows and more words: which hurt more? They kept raining on me. I was impure, unworthy because I let him seduce me. He spat on me. What do they

141

call that? I wondered. I didn't know then; now I do. Evil. That's what they call evil.

> (*She has spoken without hatred, without passion; only with sadness. And amazement.* SAM *feels he must say something to counteract the effect of her statement*)

SAM

And you believe her? How gullible you are! She says she resisted for many nights. Why didn't Berish see me with her then?

BERISH

I did!

SAM

How many times?

BERISH

Once . . . I remember it well because it was just before . . . before—

SAM

She says that I came more than once to pursue her. Really, can you see me pursue . . . her? Furthermore, if we had time, I would prove to you that I could not have been here more than once: when she says she saw me here, I was visiting friends elsewhere . . . in Marozka. Yes, the small town where our brethren were killed. I am saying this not to justify myself —I am not on trial, am I?—but to show why this woman is disqualified as a witness . . . But she is not the only one we have!

MENDEL

She is not? What do you mean?

SAM

She is young and beautiful.

BERISH

You'll die first! You won't live to set your dirty eyes on her!
(*Commotion.* BERISH *is more violent than ever.* SAM *is using the question as diversion:* MARIA*'s testimony is now forgotten*)

MENDEL

Hanna is ill. We saw her earlier. She must not be disturbed.

SAM

We are not going to hurt her, are we? We will ask her a few questions and send her back to bed. What is wrong with that?

BERISH

I'll tell you what's wrong. She's my daughter, not yours. She has seen enough criminals; I don't want her to see you, too.

SAM

Members of the court! There is one eyewitness *and* victim in this house. Isn't it our sacred duty to listen to her testimony?
(*The three judges exchange whispers*)

MENDEL

I don't understand you, Defense Attorney. Supposing we decide to summon her to the stand, surely she would help the prosecution, not the defense.

SAM

My client and I beg to differ, Your Honor. In our view, witnesses serve neither the prosecution nor the defense; they serve truth and truth alone.

BERISH

You're not going to get my daughter!

SAM

Your daughter is of no interest to this court; the witness is.

143

BERISH
You're not going to get her!

SAM

What are you afraid of? Are we not a group of respectable and honorable men—charitable, too—who would actually like nothing better than to help her and comfort her! Really, innkeeper!

BERISH

You're not going to get her!

YANKEL

Actually—

BERISH

You're not going—

AVRÉMEL

You *are* afraid!

BERISH

She is. Afraid of all men. You're not going to—

AVREMEL

Don't you trust *us*? She has seen us; she was not afraid of us.

YANKEL
(*Reassuringly*)
She will be under our protection, innkeeper. Do not worry.

AVRÉMEL

Please. Trust us. It will not last long. A minute. Please, go.

YANKEL

We would be honored to see her again.

BERISH
(*To* SAM)

You'll pay for this . . .
(*Exits, followed by* MARIA)

YANKEL

I used to like Purim.

AVRÉMEL

I loved all holidays.

MENDEL

I did not. I don't like to be told when to rejoice.

YANKEL

I do.

MENDEL

You can force yourself to accept sadness, not joy.

SAM

Is there a difference?

MENDEL

Oh, there is, Stranger, there is. (*Pause*) Haven't we two met
before? (*Pause*) Have you ever been in Zhironov? (*Pause*)
Have you ever heard of Zhironov?
(SAM *answers none of the questions. To break the uneasy
mood,* YANKEL *speaks*)

YANKEL

I have.

AVRÉMEL

The famous massacre of Zhironov. All the Jews perished
there.

MENDEL

All—except one.

YANKEL

You never told us—

AVRÉMEL

You came to us from Zhironov?

YANKEL

Were you there when—

MENDEL

Yes. I was there.

AVRÉMEL

How did you manage to escape?

SAM

There is always one singled out to escape.

YANKEL

A miracle!

SAM

There is always someone to call it a miracle.

MENDEL
(*To* SAM)

Were you there—then? No, you couldn't have been. Perhaps before? I seem to remember you in Zhironov . . .
(*Again,* SAM *does not answer. Again,* YANKEL *breaks the silence*)

YANKEL

What happened? How—

MENDEL

Sabbath morning. A crowded synagogue—more crowded than usual. I stood on the bimah before the open scrolls and read. That Shabbat we read the commandment to celebrate our holidays in joy. I had hardly finished the sentence when the doors were pushed open. The mob took over. The killers were laughing. I remember their laughter as I remember their shiny swords. Minutes later, it was all over. Not one Jew cried out; we didn't have the time. As I heard the echo of my own words: "And you shall celebrate your holidays in joy"—I found myself without a community. I was still standing; I stood throughout the slaughter. Standing before the open parchments. Why was I spared? Is it possible that they failed to see me because I was standing? I saw blood, only blood. I felt swept by madness. I whispered over and over again: "And you shall celebrate your holidays in joy, in joy, in joy." And I backed out and left.

SAM

Blessed be the Lord for His miracles.

MENDEL

A whole community was massacred, and you talk of miracles?

SAM

A Jew survived, and you ignore them?

AVRÉMEL

The mob was struck blind. How was it possible?

SAM

Miracles are miracles; they don't call for explanations.

YANKEL

They happen; they should happen more often.
    (HANNA, *in white, enters, escorted by* BERISH *and* MARIA)

MARIA

Do not be afraid, sweet little girl, do not be afraid.

HANNA

Why should I be afraid? Have you ever seen me afraid?

MARIA

No, sweet Hanna. Of course not.

HANNA

Do you know why? To show fear is to believe in misfortune.
Well, I don't.

MARIA

Of course, sweet soul. Nothing will happen. Surely not
tonight.

HANNA

Not tonight?

MARIA

Tonight is Purim.

HANNA

I wish I could play the part of Queen Esther. May I?

MARIA

Anything, sweet little Hanna. You may play anything you
wish. You may do anything you desire. We are here.

HANNA

Is she happy?

MARIA

Who?

HANNA

Esther. Queen Esther. Is she happy?

MENDEL

She must be. She is beautiful, rich, powerful; she gets what
she wants. From everybody.

HANNA

A pity.

MENDEL

A pity? Why a pity?

HANNA

I will not be able to play Queen Esther. But then, perhaps she is not happy; she only pretends.

SAM

Quite possible, young lady. I admire your charm as well as your intelligence. What you just said is possible if not probable: Esther is not happy, because she is being lied to. Everybody lies to her. The old king, her uncle, her friends. But not Haman: he doesn't lie. They all used her; not he. That makes her even more unhappy.

HANNA

Ah yes, Haman! If I play Esther, will you be Haman?

SAM

At your service, Majesty.

HANNA

Who is the king? (*To* MENDEL) You? Yes, you. And my uncle Mordechai? (*To* YANKEL) You?

YANKEL

What does he have to do?

HANNA

Be sad.

YANKEL
(*Pointing to* AVRÉMEL)

Let him be sad!

HANNA

And where are my brothers and sisters? Those that need me? Those whom I must save? Where are they? I want to see them! Their children with their innocent voices . . . their old

men with their words of wisdom . . . their brides, their grooms
. . . Where are they? Dead? Esther has not saved them. No
one has. Poor queen. Again, she was lied to.

YANKEL

But it's not in the book.

SAM

Then it's in another book.

HANNA

I don't like you.

SAM

Naturally—I am Haman. Haman does not lie. And he will
tell you something that no one is willing to admit: it's all the
queen's fault. The persecutions, the suffering, the anguish—
it's all because of her. She must have sinned many times, with
many men, to have caused such pain and so much desolation.

HANNA

But I hear music. Laughter. Shouts of happiness. I hear a
father and a mother wishing each other *mazel tov.* I hear a
voice, mine perhaps, yelling, "Arye-Leib, Arye-Leib . . ."

MENDEL

Poor Queen Esther. She remembers Hanna.

YANKEL

I want to become a judge again.

HANNA

"Arye-Leib," a voice is crying "Arye-Leib." He does not
hear, he cannot, he is dead. I am dead.

YANKEL

I demand to become a judge again!

HANNA

The queen is dead, and yet it is the most beautiful day in her life. Remember, Maria?

(HANNA *seems happy*)

BERISH

She remembers, and so do I. And I would give all that I have, my life included, to make her forget . . . They killed Arye-Leib. And his old father. And the witnesses to the wedding. And the rabbis who were about to perform the ceremony. And the musicians. The guests. They killed and killed . . . and I remember, I remember . . .

MENDEL

Go on, innkeeper. Shamgorod, Drohobitz, Zhironov, they are all alike. We must tell the tale, we must remember. Tell us everything. We shall remember.

BERISH

You have heard enough. But not all.

AVRÉMEL

I listen to you, innkeeper, and I imagine Purim without the miracle of Purim. And I know everything.

BERISH

Imagine the Jews of Shushan—and Shamgorod—mutilated, knifed, disfigured, thrown into the street, into the mud. Imagine their Queen Esther—so sweet and trusting, pure and radiant—imagine her covered with blood and dirt, imagine her lying on the floor with drunkards waiting in line . . . Can you imagine?

MENDEL

I do not have to imagine; I *know*.

MARIA

Come, Hanna. Let us go back to your room.

151

HANNA

Arye-Leib, I am so happy, Arye-Leib. We are immortal. And rich. The forest is ours. The rivers. The stars—they shine brighter. And life is calling us, as we call life. Nothing frightens us, nothing leaves us indifferent; we live at the center of the world; we are the center of the world.

MARIA
(*To the court*)

We are playing theater; but you make her suffer, and her suffering is real.

MENDEL

It's a *Purimschpiel,* Maria. You are right. Take Hanna back to her room.

HANNA

A *Purimschpiel . . .* When Purim is over, the actors remove their masks, don't they? The dead get up and the living start laughing again. When is Purim over?

(MARIA *leads her to the door and they meet the* PRIEST, *who has been standing there; he has heard* HANNA's *question*)

PRIEST

Soon, Hanna. Purim will be over very soon.

MARIA

You again?

PRIEST

I cannot sleep, Maria. This time it's not because of you. (*To the others*) Am I disturbing you again?

SAM

You never disturb us.

MARIA

Only on Purim. Except that whenever you come, it's always Purim.

PRIEST

I cannot sleep. I tried . . . Like the old king of your book, what's his name, I had bad dreams. So I decided to come back to my friend Berish and his guests.

MENDEL

You did the right thing. (*Has an idea*) Any news? Have you learned anything?

PRIEST

It's late, later than I thought. (*To* BERISH) You've refused to listen. You should have taken your daughter and your friends and fled as far away as possible. Now it's too late.

BERISH
(*With irony*)

Except, of course, if we kiss your cross—right?

PRIEST

Do not make fun of me, friend. The cross itself would no longer protect you: the killers respect it less than you do. But we could try . . .

MENDEL

Why did you come back now?

PRIEST

I don't know. To help you, of course.

MENDEL

What do you think we should do?

PRIEST

I don't know. They are too close. They are watching the inn. They are everywhere.

YANKEL

Another pogrom?

153

AVREMEL

Another trial.

MENDEL

What can we do?

PRIEST

I don't know, I'm telling you. What I do know is that
whatever you do, you must do it now.

BERISH

What you mean is—I know what you mean. Well, the answer is no. My sons and my fathers perished without betraying
their faith; I can do no less.

SAM

My dear, dear Prosecutor, you baffle me. You speak of faith,
of sacrifice, of martyrdom. Have you forgotten the trial? What
you said about my client?

PRIEST

What . . . what's that?

BERISH
(*To* SAM)

This has nothing to do with you or your client. (*Pause*) It's
a personal decision.

PRIEST

Berish, my friend Berish. You are all drunk, so am I—
perhaps. But I beg you: let's do something while there is still
time! (*Pause. He decides to have courage*) Why can't you try—I
say try—my solution temporarily? Nobody will ever know
anything about it, I swear to you. (*Has a better idea*) You know
what? Let's do it in the spirit of your Purim holiday. As a farce.
With masks. You do me a favor, and perhaps—I say perhaps
—you will stay alive; I'll handle the mob. And tomorrow,

when Purim is over, you remove the masks—and become
Jewish again. Well? What do you think, innkeeper?
    (*The three judges are flabbergasted.* HANNA *smiles*)

BERISH

I said what I had to say. My answer is no. Ask the others.
Maybe you'll have better luck with them.
    (*The* PRIEST *turns to the others. The three judges shake their
    heads*)

SAM

Thank you, Priest. Your concern touches us deeply. We are
not going to accept your solution—we all have our reasons.
Anyway, you said it yourself: the killers respect nothing.

PRIEST

So there is nothing for me to do?

MENDEL

There is something. Go to the village. Try to alert some of
your better and wiser parishioners. Get in touch with the
authorities. They may still arrive in time. Miracles are always
possible.
    (*The* PRIEST *is sad. He looks at all the characters. Tears well
    up in his eyes. He wants to shake* BERISH'*s hand but decides
    against it; will they meet again? No. But why admit it pub-
    licly? He leaves without saying a word*)

YANKEL

Is there a cellar?

AVRÉMEL

An underground passage?

MARIA

Yes, there is a cellar.

YANKEL

There must be an attic.

155

AVRÉMEL

How about making a run for it? It's still dark.

MENDEL

And the trial? The verdict?

SAM

I take note of the important fact that the prosecutor opted
for God against the enemy of God; he did so at the sacrifice
of his life. Does it mean that the case is to be dismissed?

BERISH

Not at all! I have not opted for God. I'm against His enemies, that's all.

MENDEL

So—it is going to start all over again. Jews and their enemies
will face one another once more. And then? Purim will be
over. Who will continue the thread of our tale? The last page
will not be written. But the one before? It is up to us to
prepare testimony for future generations. Thus I am asking
you for the last time: What about the trial? The verdict?

BERISH

As far as I'm concerned, the trial will go on. I haven't
changed; I'm not going to change now.

MENDEL

The end is near, and you refuse to forgive?

BERISH

I lived as a Jew, and it is as a Jew that I shall die—and it is
as a Jew that, with my last breath, I shall shout my protest to
God! And because the end is near, I shall shout louder! Because the end is near, I'll tell Him that He's more guilty than
ever!

    (MENDEL *smiles and turns to the defense attorney for his*
    final remarks)

SAM

First of all, I wish to pay tribute to the loyalty and courage of my distinguished colleague and opponent. The fact that he refused to give up his faith does him—and us—honor. As for his stubborn attitude with regard to the Almighty, of course I cannot but disagree. I understand him, but I disapprove. God is just, and His ways are just.

MENDEL

Even now?

SAM

Now and forever.

MENDEL

Just? How can anyone proclaim Him just—now? With the end so near? Look at us, look at Hanna, search your own memory: between Jews who suffer and die, and God who does not—how can you choose God?

SAM

I must. I'm His servant. He created the world and me without asking for my opinion; He may do with both whatever He wishes. Our task is to glorify Him, to praise Him, to love Him—in spite of ourselves.

MENDEL

But how *can* you?

SAM

It's simple. Faith in God must be as boundless as God Himself. If it exists at the expense of man, too bad. God is eternal, man is not.

MENDEL
(*Moves closer to him*)

Who are you, Stranger?

157

SAM

I told you. I am God's defender.

MENDEL

Who are you when you are not performing? When you are
not defending Him?

SAM

Why do you want to know?

MENDEL

Because I envy you. Your love of God: I wish I had one
measure of it. Your piety: I wish it were mine. Your faith:
mine is less profound, less intact than yours. Who are you?

SAM

I am not allowed to reveal myself to you. (*In a low voice*) And
what if I told you that I am God's emissary? I visit His creation
and bring stories back to Him. I see all things, I watch all men.
I cannot do all I want, but I can undo all things. Have I said
enough?

MENDEL

Enough for me to envy you even more. Throughout the
proceedings, you have demonstrated a respect for God that I
find admirable. And yet, we know already that God is to be
loved but also feared. In truth, if I had to pronounce a verdict
right now, it would be, I think, influenced by Berish the
innkeeper . . . But we are not going to have enough time for
our deliberations. The verdict will be announced by someone
else, at a later stage. For the trial will continue—without us.
Still, I wish I knew who you are. To follow your example.

MARIA
(*Whispering*)
You're crazy, you're all crazy . . .

MENDEL

After all, let's be frank: in the whole wide world of sorrow and agony, there was only one man, one alone, who chose to defend the honor and the glory, the justice and the kindness of God—and that was you. Who are you, Stranger? A saint? A penitent? A prophet in disguise?

MARIA

Crazy, I'm telling you . . . We're all crazy . . .

YANKEL

(*Infected by* MENDEL's *fervor*)
A wonder rabbi?

AVRÉMEL

A miracle maker?

YANKEL

An emissary sent from the kingdom of the Ten Lost Tribes?

AVRÉMEL

A mystical dreamer on his way to meet—and make us meet —the Redeemer?

YANKEL

Is this why you . . . played with Maria?

AVRÉMEL

Yes, yes: you took her so as to penetrate the depth of sin and lift up its holy sparks.
(*The door opens. The* PRIEST *reappears. From his expression, we understand: everything is lost. In the other doorway* HANNA *stands*)

BERISH

This time I'll kill. I swear to you: I'll kill.
(*They all begin building defense positions. Pushing tables to the doors. They barricade the windows.* BERISH *prepares long*

knives and hatchets. Suddenly there is collective hysteria. They all gather around SAM *and beg him to save them*)

YANKEL
(*To* SAM)
You *are* a hidden Just; intercede on our behalf!

AVRÉMEL
You are a messenger; do something!

MENDEL
You are close to heaven, pray for us! Your faith must be rewarded! Invoke it!

BERISH
I'll kill, I'll kill . . .

YANKEL
Say Psalms, holy man!

AVRÉMEL
Order the angels to come to our rescue!

YANKEL
You must accomplish miracles, you can! We know you can! Please!

AVRÉMEL
Think of Hanna—save her! Think of us—save us!

MENDEL
You are a *tzaddik,* a Just, a Rabbi, a Master—you are endowed with mystical powers; you are a holy man. Do something to revoke the decree! If you cannot, who could? You are God's only defender, you have rights and privileges: use them! For heaven's sake, use them! Oh holy man, we beg you to save God's children from further shame and suffering!
(*All candles, save one, are put out. Strange sounds are heard outside.* SAM *walks from one person to another, smiling reas-*

suringly. Then he stops before MENDEL *and scrutinizes him*)

YANKEL
It's Purim. Let's wear our masks!
(*The three judges put theirs on.* SAM *pulls his out of his pocket and raises it to his face. All shout in fear, and Satan speaks to them, laughing*)

SAM
So—you took me for a saint, a Just? Me? How could you be that blind? How could you be that stupid? If you only knew, if you only knew . . .
(*Satan is laughing. He lifts his arm as if to give a signal. At that precise moment the last candle goes out, and the door opens, accompanied by deafening and murderous roars*)

CURTAIN

AFTERWORD:
The Trial of God, The Trial of Us

by Matthew Fox

This play takes us inside the broken heart of the Polish Jewish community devastated by the pogroms of the seventeenth century and indeed inside all broken hearts and all broken communities. But it also takes us "inside the kingdom of night" of the twentieth century, the Holocaust. That is why it is rightly called a "trial of God." One might ask: Has God failed? Do the Holocaust and the other destructive events perpetrated by humanity mean that God has failed? Or has humanity failed? Or have both? Was this experiment on God's and the universe's part to pour the divine creativity and image into a two-legged species that had more in common with apes than with angels a colossal mistake? One the universe will regret forever?

Because the Jewish Biblical tradition teaches that humanity is made "in the image and likeness of God," to put God on trial is to put humanity on trial, and to put humanity on trial is to put God on trial. "All our names for God come from our understanding of ourselves" warns Meister Eckhart. To put God on trial is to put on trial our understanding of ourselves, our ways of living in the world, of denying, of accusing, of projecting, of hating, and of loving. In this play, the folly of the human condition and more, of human choices, is held up for trial. It therefore follows that the folly of God in making our species so powerful, so full of choices and creativity and power, that we can wreck evil almost godlike in its scope, is held up for trial as well.

After all, are we not the only species that is sadistic, the only species to use our immense powers of imagination to destroy one another—and which, in a sick way, gets revenge or pleasure from doing so? (In the play, the rape of Hanna is deepened in its ugliness by the perpetrators tying up her father at the scene so that he must witness it.)

This is a play about sin. If anything is sinful, it is the pogroms and the mutilations and abuses and rapes and destruction that pogroms unleash. "Sin," says Rabbi Abraham Joshua Heschel, "is the refusal of humanity to become who we are." If what we really are is an image of God, then sin is our refusal to become that image. When humans fail at this primary task—becoming Godlike, and therefore compassionate and just persons—then God dies. God fails. God gets tried for his/her failure.

The God on trial in this play is *the God made after our own image*, a God of self-righteous religion, a God of violence, a God of hatred. If the play be understood in light of our mystical tradition of letting go of all things, even of God, then everything depends on our detoxing the way we speak and talk about God, and therefore "judging" or putting on trial the gods we worship or claim to worship. What God truly occupies our hearts? Where are our true treasures and what are they? Is God implicated in the evil that humans perpetrate on one another?

This play does not present us with an abstract thesis about the nature of God or the nature of evil. Instead, it utilizes the language of art to expand and empty our hearts. It awakens *our experience of the Divine* and our *experience of the absence of the Divine*. Where was God in all this horror? Where is the good and praiseworthy Creator? Where is the God who claims to cherish his/her people?

Art is the language for expressing the mystical and the prophetic. The prophet appeals not to cognition alone but to the heart, to the gut (where injustice is first felt) and to the imagination, specifically to the moral imagination. The format chosen by Elie Wiesel, that of drama as distinct from an essay or a theological dissertation, is as significant as the play itself. For art is the most subversive—indeed prophetic—of all discourses because it speaks directly to the imagination, in this case the moral imagination and the religious imagination. Art, not theology, is the proper language for uttering our God-experience and our absence-of-God-experience. By choosing the language of drama in preference to the language of theology, Wiesel is leading us into the moral urgency of his message. An urgency that demands that we look both at our presumptions about God and our presumptions about the human species—about ourselves. The play demands that we look directly at the horrors of the history of anti-Semitism—the pogroms of past centuries—*and* at the horrors of this century. One Roman Catholic commentator who has written recently about anti-Semitism in Christianity points out that it was a pope who established the first ghettos for Jews, Pope Paul IV, in 1555. Hitler, who was a Roman Catholic and was never excommunicated, actually told a Catholic bishop that he was only doing to the Jews what the Church had done for centuries. Are the Nuremberg laws of 1935 that different from the decrees of Innocent III and Paul IV? "When the Nazis named the Jewish living-spaces 'ghettos,' they were aiming expressly to give their policies continuity with that of the popes and a species of respectability."[1]

This play does not only arouse our capacity for judging God and our notions of God and judging ourselves; it also goes deeper than judgment. It touches awe and wonder, freedom and guilt, creativity and compassion, humor and paradox. It leads us into realms of the spirit more deeply than interminable rational debate about the divine nature could ever lead us. It leads us to the experience of spirit, not only to its critique. It takes us beyond words, to the domain of silence and of holy waiting. It takes us into the holy sanctuary of sorrow. It disturbs as the spirit so often disturbs.

But silence is not all that comes forth from the players of this play. Complaint, travail, opposing personalities and ideologies and faces and forces come grinding together on this stage like great tectonic plates deep in the earth. No one emerges unscathed from this foray into history, the history of man against man, man against woman, religion against religion, man against God, God against humanity. All get confused and confounded, mixed and measured, in this grindstone that Wiesel creates as a play within a play, a history (seventeenth-century Poland) within history (our own twentieth century), history within ritual (the feast of Purim when "everything goes"). The anti-Semitism uttered by the slow-minded orthodox priest echoes our own times when we read that today—1995—48 percent of Poles believe Auschwitz was about ending the Polish state and only 8 percent understand Auschwitz to be a place where 1.5 million Jewish people were systematically murdered or eliminated. Ninety percent of the victims of Auschwitz were Jews. As Wiesel put it recently on the occasion of the fiftieth anniversary of Auschwitz's liberation, "It is true that not all the victims were Jews. But all the Jews were victims."[2]

One cries out: How much longer will anti-Semitism persist in the "Christian" West? This play does not dare to answer the question but only puts it in the most poignant way, by challenging God—as Job did—to be more impatient with human folly and injustice. It also challenges humans to be more impatient with human folly and injustice and with God's patience.

In challenging God from as many angles and arguments and personalities and religious traditions as Wiesel does in this play, he also lays bare the human capacity for seeing God anew, for moving beyond the death of God and the killing of the Divine in our midst. The God on trial in this play is no one-dimensional God, but a God who plays many roles in our personal and communitarian lives.

This play lays bare how human evil breaks our most cherished images of God. One image of God that is shattered is that of a benevolent and loving and blessing-filled God. Maria, who is a Christian, describes how life was before the pogrom.

> This was a good family, the best. Happiness was deserved and shared. Happiness, happiness. . . . Hanna's beauty—how can I describe to you Hanna's divine beauty? Whoever saw her had tears in his eyes—tears of joy and gratitude. . . . Everyone was happy, everyone thanked God for being alive to witness his own happiness. Then . . . *they* arrived. They broke everything. (p. 105)

They "broke everything," even the memory of the God of goodness. It is telling how autobiographical Wiesel's character of Hanna is as indicated in his speech on the occasion of the fiftieth anniversary of the liberation of Auschwitz. He said, "Listen to the tears of children, beautiful-looking girls among them, with golden hair, whose vulnerable tenderness never left me."[3]

Berish, Hanna's father, also had his image of God shattered by the events.

> Before, it was different—I was different. The sap of the earth enriched my own; the blood of the world flowed in my veins. I loved my steady, faithful customers. . . . To glimpse even a fleeting smile on a sad face was for me the most beautiful reward: I had to make an effort to contain my foolish tears. And God in all this? You want to hear the truth? It happened that He would touch me, on the shoulder, as if to remind me: See, Berish—I exist—I, too, exist! Then I would give Him something just to make Him happy. . . .

Berish used to experience God's touch on his shoulder. He knew the intimacy of the presence of God. All that was broken by the events, as Maria testifies when she says: "You didn't know him [Berish] before. He was generous and warm toward everybody, Jews and Christians." (p. 104)

The God-who-is-present is replaced with a God-who-is-absent. We have already seen how the traumatic gang rape that Hanna underwent rendered her mute. She, who was once beautiful with a divine beauty, is, like God, rendered mute by her experience at the hands of evil. "Something in her is silent," her father testifies; something in her speaks, weeps, remembers, and screams silently. Wiesel reports that in the trial of God held by three pious rabbis in Auschwitz that he witnessed as a boy there were only silent, dry tears. "I remember: I was there, and I felt like crying. But there nobody cried."

Not only is Hanna silenced but the entire town that was raped and pillaged and stripped of all Jews save two is silenced, as Berish testifies:

> Shamgorod is mute. Its silence—what is it if not a fact? Three houses of study—demolished, pillaged; the

main synogogue—burned down; the sacred scrolls—profaned. . . . Over a hundred Jewish familes lived here; now there is one—and this one is mutilated, maimed, deprived of joy and hope. What is all this to you—and Him?" (p. 127)

The grief, the anger, the despair—this is not just Berish's problem; it is God's problem as well. And so is the responsibility, as Berish sees it. God is implicated in the suffering of the human race. God has been silenced and allowed the Godself to be silenced. Evil has silenced God.

Mendel, who seems the wisest of the characters in this play until he is duped by Sam's rational theology, was the sole survivor of a pogrom in another city, a pogrom he witnessed in the synogogue one traumatic Sabbath morning. He had been meditating on the psalm "You shall celebrate your holidays in joy" when a mob stormed the synagogue. "Minutes later, it was all over. Not one Jew cried out; we didn't have the time. As I heard the echo of my own words: 'And you shall celebrate your holidays in joy'—I found myself without a community." (pp. 146–47)

Avremel, another of the traveling players, reports how he would go from village to village to get people to celebrate life and would rejoice to see "long, sad faces open up and become warm, good, human." Even after pogroms he would go into villages and make the living cry and the dead laugh. Mendel challenges him: "And God in all this?" Avremel answers: "I don't know. Was He laughing or crying?" (pp. 64–65) Evil confuses us as to which God we are worshipping: a laughing God or a crying God. Or an altogether absent God.

Berish was stripped of his former person and personality by the grief and pain he had undergone. He testifies: "Since that night I am no longer the same person. That night, life stopped flowing. Nothing matters any more. Nothing exists. Berish is alive, but I am not him. Life goes on but outside me, away from me. . . . Before, it was different—I was different." (pp. 44–45) Before the evil event, he knew the God of blessing. Now, no longer. Berish, like Job, has been stripped of everything and now tastes nothingness.

Mendel, Yankel, and Avremel all sing a song of lament, a song of *un*praise, for the Creator who seems to have been banished by the pain and suffering in the world.

> Misery of miseries . . . In the whole world, from east to west, from south to north, is there no one to plead on behalf of the Almighty? No one to speak for Him? . . . . No one to justify His ways? . . . No one to sing His glory? . . . In the entire creation, from kingdom to kingdom and nation to nation, is there not one person to be found, one person to take the side of the Creator? Not one believer to explain His mysteries? Not one teacher to love Him in spite of everything, and love Him enough to defend Him against His accusers? Is there no one in the whole universe who would take the case of the Almighty God? (p. 109)

Here we see God being stripped of the power of creation, the glory and joy and blessedness of creation. A God without creation to boast of. A God without defenders. A God totally immersed in the darkness and nothingness humans experience as the "dark night of the soul," the mystical term for our times of deep pain and anguish and nothingness. One voice speaks up, that of a stranger who we later know as Sam. And as Satan. God's only defender.

Berish attributes responsibility for suffering to God, while Sam seems to typify the perfect academic theologian who solves everything and knows all about God. Consider the following exchange. Mendel confronts Sam: "You are not even awed? You feel nothing?" Sam responds: "I dislike emotions. I prefer facts and cool logic." (p. 122) This suggests that evil begins in our forgetfulness of awe, our forgetfulness of blessing and the passion for existence. Sam is incapable of experiencing awe. He talks about praising but he does not praise. What Rabbi Heschel calls "radical amazement" does not touch Sam.

Maria, who is the only one who sees through Sam, says of him: "He has no heart, no soul, no feeling! He's Satan, I'm telling you! . . . He is evil. Cruel. He's not human. I'm telling you, he's not human." (pp. 116–17) And again, "Evil. That's what they call evil." (p. 142) Evil according to Maria is being without pathos, without feeling and passion and empathy and compassion. While her opinion of Sam is ignored by the men, at the end of the play, hers is the only judgment that endures. Sam has duped the men with his verbal excellence and his ability to utter shibboleth upon shibboleth about the God they recognize. Sam is at home speaking in absolutes. He says: "I'm His servant. He created the world and me without asking for my opinion; He may do with both whatever He wishes. Our task is to glorify Him, to praise Him, to love Him—in spite of ourselves. . . . Faith in God must be as boundless as God Himself. If it exists at the expense of man, too bad. God is eternal, man is not." (p. 157)

So taken in are the men by Sam's eloquence and rationality that they look to him as redeemer in the very last scene of the play . . . until the very last moment, when Sam's intentions are exposed.

Berish gets to the heart of our humanity and morality when he declares that "to be free means to be able to choose." (p. 65) The act of choosing is the act of creativity and the act of creativity is our act of choice. In the play there is much going back and forth in an effort to choose a defender for God. Perhaps the fact that the players can't choose suggests that they are not free. This lack of decision and will to make a choice frustrates the audience, so that we, too, enter into this state of limited creativity. The image of the God of creativity, and therefore morality, has been shattered.

The God of justice and compassion is also shattered. Where was the God of justice and the compassion of God during the pogroms, during the Holocaust? Is God not on the side of the oppressed? Or is God on the side of the oppressor? These questions are raised when Berish declares:

> I don't want a minor, secondary justice, a poor man's justice! I want no part of a justice that escapes me, di-

minishes me and makes a mockery out of mine! Justice is here for men and women—I therefore want it to be human, or let Him keep it! . . . Why shouldn't the victims of injustice take part in a debate over justice? (p. 123)

Sam pronounces a familiar shibbolith about God's justice when he says, "God is just and His ways are just." But Mendel replies, "Just? How can anyone proclaim Him just—now? With the end so near? Look at us, look at Hanna, search your own memory: between Jews who suffer and die, and God who does not—how can you choose God?" (p. 157) Berish rejects the idea that God was a victim in the moment of evil. "He—a victim? A victim is powerless; is He powerless? He is almighty, isn't He? He could use His might to save the victims, but He doesn't! So —on whose side is He? Could the killer kill without His blessing—without His complicity? . . . He is not on the side of the victim. . . . The witnesses for the prosecution are the dead. All of them." (p. 129) And again, he insists: "Don't talk to me of His suffering—leave that to the priest. If I am given the choice of feeling sorry for Him or for human beings, I choose the latter anytime. He is big enough, strong enough to take care of Himself; man is not." (p. 133) One can propose that Wiesel is underscoring that there has been too much emphasis in Christianity on the suffering God—and not enough emphasis on suffering humanity.

This play may be less about putting God on trial than about putting our uses and abuses and projections of God on trial. As such, it liberates and redeems, much as the Exodus event liberated and redeemed our spiritual ancestors. It is about trying our idols and holding them up to examination. Not only is a one-dimensional idea of God erased in the play, but so, too, is a one-dimensional notion of evil, and even of Satan himself, eliminated. Satan's sublety is so deep that he seduces the entire cast except Maria, whom he has seduced earlier—into his logic and common sense. And, paradoxically, he is sometimes right and sometimes wrong in his opinions. Evil is no mere *pri-*

vatio boni in this play. It plays an active role—as the defender of God—indeed God's *only* defender. It plays a role as the Great Denial.

Satan sounds oh so theologically correct and logical. He could get a job in most academic theological institutions today. Beware of theologians and excessive rationalizations, Wiesel is warning. Rightly so. For theology too easily strays into the lap of the left brain, too far from the guts where injustice as well as compassion are felt and where wonder and amazement are tasted.

One theme that Berish repeats on several occasions is the idea that God is on the side of the killers because they believe he is. There is a strong statement offered by Mendel about the injustice done Christ by Christians and Christianity; that Christianity has hardly anything to do with the following of Christ:

> I speak not of Christ but of those who betray Him. They invoke His teaching to justify their murderous deeds. His true disciples would behave differently; there are no more around. There are no more Christians in this Christian land. (p. 99)

But can God be redeemed? Is the God who allows such horrors to happen worthy of redemption? These are the disturbing and radical questions raised by this play. Of course, the responses hinge a great deal on what sort of God we are praising and honoring and remembering. Meister Eckhart, a mystic and prophetic figure of the late thirteenth and early fourteenth century who supported oppressed peasants and women in his day, used to say, "I pray God to rid me of God." In many ways that is what I heard echoed in this trial of God: it was a trial to finally rid ourselves of a God who is too small, who does not live up to the divine nature of compassion and justice, who has not penetrated the lives of his/her followers, who allows the Godself to be used for programs and pogroms of racism, injustice, genocide, hatred, murder, and ignorance. Religious fanatics are prophets with no love, prophets with no mystical soul. They are false prophets, therefore, and corrupters of true religion. While those who dissent are often the true prophets.

The purpose of a trial is to determine justice, so in the context of *The Trial of God*, justice is the issue of the entire play. Yet, no decision is rendered. Berish, however, dissents from the refusal to decide. He has come to his own conclusions about God's guilt or innocence:

> I—Berish, Jewish innkeeper at Shamgorod—accuse Him of hostility, cruelty and indifference. Either He dislikes His chosen people or He doesn't care about them—period! . . . Either He knows what's happening to us, or He doesn't wish to know! In both cases He is . . . guilty! Yes, guilty! (p. 125)

Even at the end, with the killers at the door, Berish remains true to his Jewishness and to his opinion about God's absence. Therefore his rage continues:

> I lived as a Jew, and it is as a Jew that I shall die—and it is as a Jew that, with my last breath, I shall shout my protest to God! And because the end is near, I shall shout louder! Because the end is near, I'll tell Him that He's more guilty than ever! (p. 156)

This play has much in common with the book of Job which raised the same basic questions: Why do good people suffer? Where is God in all this? Where is justice? In the Book of Job no definitive answer is given but there is a passage in which God admonishes Job to become less anthropocentric and to see human suffering in the larger context of the creation itself.

Where were you, Job, when I laid the foundation of the earth?
Tell me if you have understanding.
Who determined its measurements—surely you know . . .
Or who shut in the sea with doors, when it burst forth
   from the womb?
Have you commanded the morning or caused the dawn
   to know its place?
Have you comprehended the expanse of the earth?
Declare if you know all this.
Can you hunt the prey for the lion?
Do you know how the mountain goats bring forth?
Do you give the horse its might?

(Job 38: 4–12)

God's response to Job's grief and anger at his suffering is to challenge Job anew with the amazement and wonder of the universe and to suggest that it is in that cosmological context that Job must understand his fate and learn from it. Job replies:

I am speechless: what can I answer?
   I put my hand on my mouth.
I have said too much already;
   now I will speak no more.

(Job 40: 4–5)

Awe returns, as does the silence that comes when we let go of anthropocentrism and rediscover God's whole creation.

I read recently of a Holocaust survivor who said that no matter what the Nazis were doing at night they had no control over the sun, and that even on the worst of days from the point of view of human evil going on in the camps, the sunlight might break through a board in the barracks. In spite of human cruelty and evil, the God of the sun and the moon and the trees and the soil was still at work. Even today, after the Holocaust, trees still grow and provide paper for playwrights to tell their stories on and for construction workers to build theaters with. Ears and hearts develop so that listening and remembering is possible.

Life goes on. As Rilke put it, "existence for us is the miracle." Existence *is* a miracle. A holy miracle. That is why robbing another of it is so evil a deed. It is a sacrilege. And so the miracle of existence is our mysticism, our response to the God of grace and beauty and goodness and blessing.

But resistance is also a miracle. It is the miracle of paying attention to moral outrage and responding to it. It is the miracle that connects all prophets and the prophetic spirit in all women and men. It is human evidence that the God who promises justice and compassion is still alive, alive in his/her holy ones. In those who refuse to let us forget the evil that so readily captures human imagination and human works. Existence and Resistance. These are the evidences of the Divine presence, however silent that presence sometimes appears to be. God is alive on earth only to the extent that God's works and creatures are alive. God exists and God resists to the extent that humans do both in the name of God.

So great is humanity's capacity for evil that the God of justice is indeed silenced by humanity's evil deeds—but the God of the sun and moon and stars, of time and space and the fifteen billion years that brought humanity into being, the God of life itself, of the horses and lions and mountain goats that caught Job's attention—that God is not silenced. The God of the cosmos is not silenced.

Intervention or nonintervention: that seems to be the religious dilemma posed by players in this play as well as Job, and indeed in the Christian story as well. Maybe growing up religiously means moving from an exclusively *interventionist* theology of redemption to a *coresponsibility* theology of redemption. In the former we are taught to await salvation *from the outside* (much like the men in the play, who kept looking for Sam to deliver them right up to the end). Such a theology presumes a theistic world view; that is, that the God of creation and liberation is *outside of things*. In a *coresponsibility* theology of redemption God is not seen theistically or outside of things but panentheistically or within things and with things within God. Redemption in this context would be less about outside interventions than about humans waking up to their own responsibility and power as communities, as individuals, and as a species, to stand up and say "No!"

Such redemption includes humanity's responsibility to give birth to alternatives. To listen so deeply to the grief and pain caused by human sin and folly that we simply find it unacceptable and turn to other ways of being human. Or, if you will, in the spirit of Heschel, other ways to become who we are. Ways to be cocreators with a suffering God, a God who feels the pathos of our condition but is decidedly not patient with the human folly that is the cause of much of it.

We humans are still incredulous when we hear how much responsibility we bear for our own fate and that of others. Is it God we don't believe in, or ourselves as images of God? If we believed in the latter, our ways would have to change.

A God of cocreation and coresponsibility has created a species destined for cocreation and coresponsibility. Such a God is a God still waiting impatiently for us humans to start playing our proper role in creation and redemption. Holy impatience. Ours are times for a holy impatience. For the Holocaust of the twentieth century, like the pogroms of the seventeenth, may be a mere prelude to the potential collective acts of evil that the human species is capable of in the twenty-first century: acts of genocide and biocide on an even larger scale. If we fail to make the spiritual leaps and jumps that are long overdue for our species, subsequent generations—if there are any—will be justified in putting our God and gods on trial. Or, as Mendel puts it in this play, "We are not going to have enough time for our deliberations. The verdict will be announced by someone else, at a later stage. For the trial will continue—without us."

And so the trial goes on. God's trial. Our trial. The image of God on trial. And time is running out.

Matthew Fox
Professor of Spirituality
Institute in Culture and Creation Spirituality
Holy Names College
Oakland, California
April 1995

Notes

[1] Peter de Rosa, *Vicars of Christ* (New York: Crown Publishers, 1988), p. 196.

[2] Elie Wiesel, "Close Your Eyes, and Listen to the Silent Screams," *The Sunday Times* (London), January 29, 1995, p. 3.

[3] Wiesel, "Close Your Eyes," p. 3.

BOOKS BY

Elie Wiesel

Available from Schocken

A BEGGAR IN JERUSALEM

In the days following the Six-Day War, a Holocaust survivor visits the reunited city of Jerusalem. At the Western Wall he encounters the beggars and madmen who congregate there every evening, and who force him to confront the ghosts of his past and his ties to the present.

THE FORGOTTEN

Distinguished psychotherapist and Holocaust survivor Elhanan Rosenbaum is losing his memory to an incurable disease. Never having spoken of the war years before, he resolves to tell his son about his past—the heroic parts as well as the parts that fill him with shame—before it is too late.

FROM THE KINGDOM OF MEMORY

The essays and speeches collected here include reminiscences of Wiesel's life before the Holocaust and his struggle to find meaning afterward, his impassioned testimony at the Klaus Barbie trial, his plea to President Reagan not to visit a German S. S. cemetery, and his speech in acceptance of the Nobel Peace Prize.

THE GATES OF THE FOREST

A young Jew hiding from the Nazis in the forests and small towns of Eastern Europe allows another refugee to sacrifice himself in his stead. As he struggles with his guilt, one questions recurs: How to live in a world that God has abandoned?

LEGENDS OF OUR TIME

From a rabbi at Auschwitz who fasts on Yom Kippur, to a young Spanish Catholic whose discovery of an ancient Marrano document starts him on a quest to regain his lost heritage, Wiesel's encounters with fifteen extraordinary men and women resonate with the poetry and passion of Jewish spiritual resistance.

THE TOWN BEYOND THE WALL

Based on Wiesel's own life, this is the story of a young Holocaust survivor who returns to his hometown, seeking to understand the mystery of what he calls "the face in the window"—the symbol of those who stood by and watched as innocent men, women, and children were led to the slaughter.

THE TRIAL OF GOD

When three itinerant actors arrive in a small Eastern European village, they are horrified to discover that all but two of the Jewish residents have been murdered in a recent pogrom. The actors decide to stage a mock trial of God, indicting Him for allowing such things to happen to His children.

TWILIGHT

The story of a man whose search for the friend who saved him during the Holocaust leads him to question the very meaning of survival, this novel of memory, loss, and madness resonates with the dramatic upheavals of our century.

Available from Vintage

A JEW TODAY

In this powerful collection of essays, letter, and diary entries, Wiesel probes such central moral and political issues as Zionism and the Middle East conflict, anti-Semitism in the former U.S.S.R., the obligations of American Jews toward Israel, and the media's treatment of the Holocaust.

AVAILABLE AT YOUR LOCAL BOOKSTORE *or*

To order by mail, please fill out or copy the form below and send to:
Random House Order Department,
400 Hahn Road, Westminster, Maryland 21157.
To order by phone, call 1-800-733-3000 (credit cards only).

- If you wish to pay by check or money order, please make it payable to Random House, Inc.
- If you prefer to charge your order to a major credit card, please fill in the information below.

Charge my account with
❑ American Express ❑ Visa ❑ MasterCard

Account No._____ Expiration Date _____

(Signature)_____

Name _____

Address _____

City/State/Zip _____

TITLE	ISBN	QUANTITY	PRICE	TOTAL
A Beggar in Jerusalem	0-8052-0897-6	_____ x	$14.00	= _____
The Forgotten	0-8052-1019-9	_____ x	$14.00	= _____
From The Kingdom of Memory	0-8052-1020-2	_____ x	$14.00	= _____
The Gates of the Forest	0-8052-1044-X	_____ x	$13.00	= _____
A Jew Today	0-394-74057-2	_____ x	$ 9.00	= _____
Legends of Our Time	0-8052-0714-7	_____ x	$14.00	= _____
The Town Beyond the Wall	0-8052-1045-8	_____ x	$13.00	= _____
The Trial of God	0-8052-1053-9	_____ x	$12.00	= _____
Twilight	0-8052-1058-X	_____ x	$12.00	= _____

Shipping/Handling* = _____

Subtotal = _____

Sales Tax (where applicable) = _____

Total Enclosed = $_____

*In addition to the price of the books, enclose shipping and handling: $2.00 for the first book and $0.50 for each additional book ordered.
Prices subject to change without notice. Please allow 4-6 weeks for delivery.

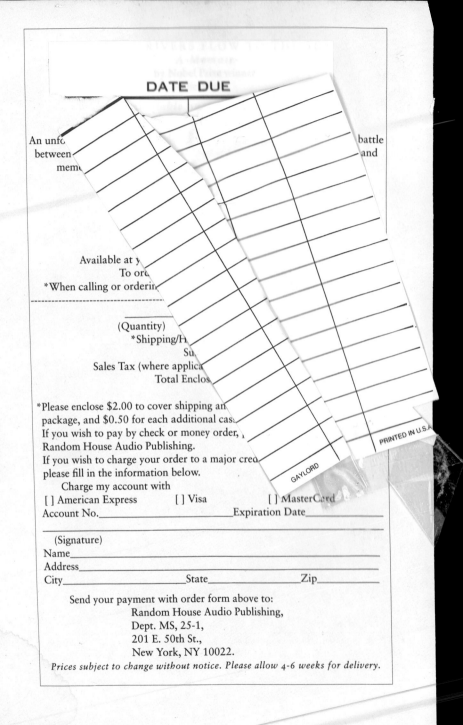

DATE DUE

An unfo   battle
between   and
mem

Available at y
To or
*When calling or orderin

(Quantity)
*Shipping/H
Su
Sales Tax (where applica
Total Enclos

*Please enclose $2.00 to cover shipping an
package, and $0.50 for each additional cas
If you wish to pay by check or money order,
Random House Audio Publishing.
If you wish to charge your order to a major cred
please fill in the information below.
     Charge my account with
[ ] American Express   [ ] Visa   [ ] MasterCard
Account No._____Expiration Date_____
_____
     (Signature)
Name_____
Address_____
City_____State_____Zip_____

Send your payment with order form above to:
          Random House Audio Publishing,
          Dept. MS, 25-1,
          201 E. 50th St.,
          New York, NY 10022.
Prices subject to change without notice. Please allow 4-6 weeks for delivery.

PRINTED IN U.S.A

GAYLORD